THE MYSTIC SEPULCHRE

THE MYSTIC SEPULCHRE;

or,

SUCH THINGS HAVE BEEN.

A Spanish Romance.

JOHN PALMER, Jun.

" 'TWAS BUT MY FANCY!"—
King Richard the Third.

Edited and with an introduction by
Joel T. Terranova

VALANCOURT BOOKS

First published London: W. Earle, 1806
First Valancourt Books edition 2020

Introduction, Notes, and Note on the Text copyright © 2020 by
Joel T. Terranova

Published by Valancourt Books, Richmond, Virginia
http://www.valancourtbooks.com

ISBN 978-1-948405-48-5 (trade paperback)
Also available as an electronic book.

Set in Dante MT

CONTENTS

INTRODUCTION

If the life of John Palmer, Jun. (1776-1809) were to be adapted as a play, it would most likely focus on the life-long disappointment and struggle of its central character. Indeed, Palmer's relatively short life is an embodiment of the term 'tragedy' in nearly every sense of the word.

The oldest son of a famed London actor, John Palmer (1744-1798), the younger Palmer followed in his father's footsteps as an actor in the hopes of achieving a level of success that would enable him to earn a living. First appearing with his father on stage during a production of Shakespeare's *Henry IV, Part One* (1597) in 1791, Palmer nonetheless failed to demonstrate he was the heir to his father's stage talents after a few years as an actor and he later decided to try his hand as a novelist instead. In 1795, he published his first work, *The Haunted Cavern: A Caledonian Tale*, which proved successful in terms of the attention it received and its popularity with readers. One can imagine that Palmer was, at this point, emboldened to replicate this accomplishment, for the following year he published his second novel, *The Mystery of the Black Tower*. This text proved successful for Palmer, though not quite nearly on the same scale as *The Haunted Cavern* had been. During the next thirteen years of his life, Palmer wrote three more novels: *The World as it Goes; or, Portraits from Nature* (1803), *The Mystic Sepulchre; or, Such Things Have Been. A Spanish Romance* (1806), and *Like Master Like Man: A Novel* (published posthumously in 1811). He also continued acting wherever he could, in the hopes of earning income for his family, as evidenced in an 1807 review of his acting talents, included in the appendix of this edition.

When Palmer passed away in 1809, he left a sickly wife with no money or means to survive financially. George Colman the Younger (1762-1836), playwright and manager of the theatre at Haymarket, took notice of her plight and proposed to the London publisher William Earle that the proceeds of *Like Master Like Man* be used to help Palmer's widow; Earle agreed to Colman's proposal. In the introduction to Palmer's final novel, Colman paints a woeful image of Palmer as one whom lasting success never visited in his labors as an actor and novelist. Palmer, according to Colman, struggled to support himself and his wife, but was never able to do more then to take care of their most urgent needs.

Three years before his death, Palmer published his fourth novel, *The Mystic Sepulchre*, with the hope that it would be a modest success as *The Haunted Cavern* had been —it was anything but successful despite a reissue in 1807. *The Mystic Sepulchre* was a gamble on Palmer's part. During the 1790s, when he published both *The Haunted Cavern* and *The Mystery of the Black Tower*, the Gothic romance was at the peak of its popularity with the British reading public. Yet popular literary tastes are often fickle and by 1806 the Gothic had lost much of its appeal with readers. According to Robert Miles, in "The 1790s: The Effulgence of Gothic", there "is a sharp increase in Gothic 'product' starting in 1788, followed by a further upward deflection point in 1793. From 1788 until 1807 the Gothic maintains a market share of around 30 percent of novel production, reaching a high point of 38 percent in 1795, then dipping to around 20 percent in 1808" (42). Given this important change in the literary marketplace, then, Palmer had published his final gothic romance a bit too late for it to have met with any form of commercial success with the waning of the Gothic romance's popularity. Despite this unfortunate change in literary taste, Palmer's *The Mystic Sepulchre* nonetheless exemplifies the conventions of the early Gothic romance and why readers at the end of the eighteenth century found the genre so enticing.

As its full title indicates, *The Mystic Sepulchre* takes place in Spain during the reign of Ferdinand and Isabella (1474-1504). Both monarchs feature in the plot as minor characters, as does the Spanish Inquisition as a powerful political force. However, this is as far as Palmer takes the historicization of this particular work, a staunch departure from his previous two Gothic romances, which are characterized by their strong use of history. Instead, Palmer demonstrates almost complete concern with situation and description in *The Mystic Sepulchre*. As with many of the Gothic romances of the 1790s, the characters and plot of this text are expected stocks that any experienced Gothic reader would have previously encountered. Palmer, however, shows substantial growth as a practitioner of the Gothic romance when dealing with the aesthetics of atmosphere and mood here over his earlier works. He is more focused and intricate in his use of description, and the Gothic elements of this work are effectively utilized in a manner that is pleasing to the reader. While there are certainly problems with the narrative, such as the distracting subplot involving Lord Liffey, that detract from the unity of the text, *The Mystic Sepulchre* nonetheless proves a delight to the reader who approaches the text for its Gothic offerings as Palmer proves more than capable in offering the sort of novel that the reading public flocked to a decade earlier.

The Mystic Sepulchre was the last of Palmer's novels published during his lifetime. His literary career had begun with promising success but ultimately failed to materialize into anything of lasting significance in the way he had hoped for. Yet Palmer proved himself a capable practitioner of the Gothic romance with his first novel and demonstrated an ability to improve his skills with each subsequent effort. *The Mystic Sepulchre*, then, stands as a minor Gothic romance that succeeds as a specimen of its genre. It proves a delightful experience for those who enjoy the fright and tension offered by the Gothic.

JOEL T. TERRANOVA, PH.D.
Lafayette, Louisiana

FURTHER READING

Primary Sources

Palmer, John. *The Haunted Cavern: A Caledonian Tale*. Edited by Joel T. Terranova. Richmond: Valancourt Books, 2013.
—. *The Mystery of the Black Tower*. 1796. Edited by James D. Jenkins. Chicago: Valancourt Books, 2005.

Secondary Sources

Birkhead, Edith. *The Tale of Terror: A Study of the Gothic Romance*. 1921.

Clery, E. J. *The Rise of Supernatural Fiction, 1762-1800*. Cambridge: Cambridge University Press, 1995.

Crawford, Joseph. *Gothic Fiction and the Invention of Terrorism: The Politics and Aesthetics of Fear in the Age of the Reign of Terror*. London: Bloomsbury, 2013.

Ellis, Markman. *The History of Gothic Fiction*. Edinburgh: Edinburgh University Press, 2000.

Frank, Frederick S. *The First Gothics: A Critical Guide to the English Gothic Novel*. New York: Garland, 1987.

Kilgour, Maggie. *The Rise of the Gothic Novel*. London: Routledge, 1995.

Miles, Robert. "The 1790s: The Effulgence of Gothic." *The Cambridge Companion to Gothic Fiction*. Edited by Jerrold E. Hogle. Cambridge: Cambridge University Press, 2002. 41-62.

Punter, David. *The Literature of Terror: The Gothic Tradition*. 2nd ed. London: Longman, 1996.

Railo, Eino. *The Haunted Castle: A Study of the Elements of English Romanticism*. 1927. New York: Humanities Press, 1964.

Varma, Devendra P. *The Gothic Flame*. New York: Russell & Russell, 1966.

A NOTE ON THE TEXT

The Mystic Sepulchre was the fourth of Palmer's published novels, appearing in print just two years before his death in 1809 at the age of thirty-three. It was published in London by W. Earle in 1806. In 1807, *The Mystic Sepulchre* was apparently reissued by Earle, who would also later publish Palmer's final novel, *Like Master Like Man*, after Palmer's death, for the benefit of his widow. While *The Mystic Sepulchre* was the third of Palmer's three gothic romances, it seems to have been met with little to no interest by the reading public. There are no known contemporary reviews of it despite several periodicals, such as *The Athenaeum* and *The Edinburgh Review*, announcing it as a new publication. This is far from the attention surrounding his first published novel, *The Haunted Cavern*, which received seven reviews of varying opinions just twelve years earlier. In 1810, *The Mystic Sepulchre* was translated into French and published under the title *Le tombeau mysterieux, ou Les familles de Henarez et d'Almanza: roman espagnol*. Aside from the 1807 reissue and the 1810 French edition, *The Mystic Sepulchre* was never republished and the existing scholarship that references it has been limited to bibliographic entries.

This edition remains faithful to the original 1806 edition. I have silently corrected various errors made by both Palmer and the publisher. The language has been not been modernized and I have only made alterations to words that are clearly misspelled. Some punctuation has been simplified in instances where it becomes excessive and confusing. My goal here has been to preserve the flavor of the text as it was first published but to also ensure it is an enjoyable experience for the twenty-first-century reader.

I have provided footnotes for the reader's reference regarding the literary sources that Palmer quotes in the epigraphs and elsewhere. Footnotes have also been provided for problematic passages where Palmer has confused a character with another; in such cases, I have corrected the character's name and provided a footnote that explains the error.

Special thanks are due to Troy Hoffpauir for his assistance with this project in its early stages. Without his support, I question whether this edition would have been completed as soon as it was.

I would also like to thank the staff of the British Library and Dupre Library at the University of Louisiana at Lafayette for their help with various matters that arose during my work on this edition of *The Mystic Sepulchre*.

THE

MYSTIC SEPULCHRE;

OR,

SUCH THINGS HAVE BEEN.

A Spanish Romance.

IN TWO VOLUMES.

By JOHN PALMER,

Author of the " Haunted Cavern"—" Mystery of the Black Tower"—" World as it goes," &c.

" 'TWAS BUT MY FANCY !"—

King Richard the Third.

VOL. I.

London.

Printed by J. NICHOLS, Earl's-conrt, Leicester Square.

FOR W. EARLE,

ALBEMARLE-STREET, PICCADILLY,

. . . .

1807.

CHAP. I.

Blow, blow, thou winter-wind!
Thou art not so unkind
As man's ingratitude!—

AS YOU LIKE IT.[1]

———— Poor wretch!
That for thy mother's fault art thus expos'd!

THE WINTER'S TALE[2]

THE night was dark—the foaming water-fall rushed down the rugged mountain's side, in awful grandeur—loud roared the thunder—vivid slashed the lightning—fast fell the sheeted rain—and the angry wind howled round his head—as slowly journeyed the weary Carlos on his cheer-less way. Oft did he cast an anxious look around, in search of some habitation; but in vain—not being able, so far as his eye could pierce, to discern any thing but the brown heath of the Sierra Morena o'er which he past, with here and there a few scattered cork-trees, and the dusky and imperfect shade of some o'er-hanging precipice. Now and then the moon suddenly emerged from the black clouds of a lowering sky, and instantly retired again; having just served to give the forlorn traveller a more extensive view of his wretched situation. Hope, and native courage awhile, urged him to push forward, but the increasing storm, and his fatigue of body and mind, at length, overcame him, he

1 William Shakespeare (1564-1616), *As You Like It* (1623), 2.7.174-176.
2 Shakespeare, *The Winter's Tale* (1623), 3.3.48-49.

dreaded to move from the spot whereon he stood, from the apprehension of unknown pits and precipices, and cast himself in a transport of despair upon the earth. There he had not long continued, when a faint cry struck upon his ear: he started up, and listened; but in vain—the sound was hushed—and he was once more about to throw himself on the damp ground, when the same feeble plaint was repeated.—He cast a glance towards the spot whence the sounds seemed to issue; but the moon was enveloped in vapours, and refused to assist his search. Nothing discouraged, he advanced, determined to yield what aid he might be able to do, when a flash of lightning discovered a basket at his feet.

He opened it, and found an infant curiously nestled within.

"Merciful God!" he exclaimed, with a mingled sensation of horror, pity, and surprise; "What find I here? What wretch, divested of humanity, could own an heart callous enough, thus to expose thy hapless innocence!—Alas! miserable that I am! little did I think in this sequestered spot to find a partner in affliction—much less, in one so tender —so undeserving of the frowns of fortune, as thou art! —But, pretty babe! whatever be the unhappy Carlos' lot, thou shalt be his first care; and if he forget to cherish and protect thee, may heaven forget him, in his utmost need, and the retribution due to thy accursed persecutors."

A tear rolled down his manly cheek, as he pressed his lips to those of the infant, whom he, with much care, wrapped within his cloak, and recommenced his course—in which he had not proceeded far, when the moon-beams disclosed to his anxious gaze, the mist-clad turrets of a lofty edifice.

"Blessed sight!" cried the wanderer. "If hospitality be housed within yon mansion, a portion of it will surely be granted to the way-worn passenger!"

On gaining the building, he found it to be a stupendous gothic castle, surrounded by a moat. He crossed the draw-bridge, (whose crazy planks tottered beneath his tread) which led him to the outer court. He traversed the front, with slow and cautious steps. All was silent.

At length, he seized the massy knocker, and struck upon the great gate; the sound reverberated, and silence once more ensued: he struck again, but to no purpose; and a third time—when a hoarse voice, from within, demanded: "Who's there?"

"A traveller, worn by fatigue, and drenched with the storm, entreats the shelter of your roof, till dawn," quoth Carlos.

"Why, you must have the impudence of the devil, to make this rattle at a nobleman's gate, at midnight!—But you must travel on, Signor Traveller! for small is the shelter you get here."

"I beg, I beseech you, to grant me a lodging!" said Carlos. "Not on my own account; but for the sake of the tender burden which I bear."

"Burden!" repeated the fellow within, "a pedlar, I suppose, or more likely a sturdy thief. But I have nothing to do with that: you and your burden may go to the devil together—for you don't come in here."

Carlos swelled with indignation; but the situation of his tender charge, for whom he yet hoped to obtain an asylum, restrained the anger of his tongue, and he once more sought to assail the ruffian's feelings.

"As you shall hope for mercy from above, bestow it now!" said he. "I have an infant in my arms, half dead with cold and hunger. Have pity on the babe if you have none on me: let it not perish for the succour you have it in your power to bestow."

"None of your flourishes!" returned the brute. "Your

smooth speeches won't do here; for if you and your brat die at the door together, you may for me."

"Eternal father!" cried Carlos, "is it possible that one, on whom thou hast bestowed thine own celestial image, should thus degrade his nature?—come on, sweet innocent! some shed, if such I haply can discover, must now be thy rude tenement."

He bent his steps from the inhospitable mansion, and had re-measured half the drawbridge, when the repeated moans of the child struck to his heart.

"Let come what may," thus spoke he, to himself, "I will make one more effort for admission!"

He returned; and, grasping the knocker, struck, with full force, upon the portal.

"What, are you there again?" cried the savage within. "I thought, I had given you an answer before. But mark me! if you don't move off, and that quickly too—I shall add the weight of a brace of bullets to your burden; which you may not find quite so convenient to carry away with you."

"Beshrew thee for an inhuman varlet!" cried a feeble voice from a window over the gate. "I would with all my soul, thou hadst a brace now quivering in thy grumbling gizzard!—Tarry stranger, I will give thee admittance, and refreshment too, by Saint Iago!"

Presently the door was unbarred; and an old man in a night-cap and gown, with a lamp in his hand appeared.

"Well, Master Lewis," said the fellow, who first accosted Carlos, "if any harm come of this, you must bear the blame. You can't accuse me."—

"Of humanity?" interrupted the old man. "By Saint Iago! you say true, for once; 'tis a failing of which thou wilt never be even suspected. Were your gate as hard to open as your heart, you'd have a plaguy troublesome post of it,

Master *Cerberus*. But, follow me, courteous stranger; and I will see whether the castle of Henares cannot furnish somewhat to comfort thee, withal."

Carlos accompanied Lewis (so was his conductor called) to the kitchen; when the old man threw a log of wood on the back of the expiring embers; and, apologizing for having ushered him there, as the only room wherein there was any fire, assured him, he should speedily have refreshment.

"I care not for myself; I have suffered too much, within, to heed the pitiless pelting of the storm, or the cries of hunger," said Carlos. "But, for this innocent" (and he threw his cloak from about the child) "I beg some speedy nutriment."

"Aha! is it so Signor Cavalier?" cried the old man. "I warrant me, (Saint Iago be her speed!) some credulous damsel is bewailing her folly now. I remember when I was a younker (and a gay spark I was) I remember I got on the blind side of one-eyed Tabitha, daughter to Bazil, the broken-backed barber of Barcelona.—I wheedled—and I pressed—and I ——, but it's no matter—it's all over with me now!"

"I will affect ignorance of your drift," quoth Carlos, "but you suspect me wrongfully. Upon the honor of a Spaniard, this child being with me is the mere effect of chance!"

"Well, well," cried Lewis, "you are not the first cavalier whose lot has been to have a *chance*-child. Be that as it may, I will fetch one to take charge of the bantling.—Ha! ha! ha! A chance-child, quotha!—By Saint Iago! Signor, you're a wag!"

So saying, Lewis left the kitchen; whither he soon returned, accompanied by an old woman, whose appearance filled Carlos with disgust. Her skin was shrivelled, and appeared as if it had been rubbed with walnut-shells—

her eyes were red and spiteful—her nose enormous—and her mouth retained a few teeth, whose alternate black and white resembled the keys of an harpsichord. Her head was covered with a black-cap, secured under the chin by a hood of crimson cloth; so that the *tout ensemble*, was that of a fury, rather than of one of mortal mould.

"In the name of the virgin! why am I disturbed in my sleep, at this late hour?" grumbled the hog. "Marry come up! we shall have all the children in the province brought to us, at this rate, I trow!—Indeed, Signor Lewis, I can't think what you were about to—"

"No matter what," said Lewis. "Perhaps, I had not forgot that I was once young myself; and, who knows, you and I may have received a kindness, similar to the one we are going to bestow?—You understand me, Leonarda!"

"I scorn your scurrility!" cried she. "My virtue has been as pure as Pyrenean mountain-snow, and as hard to come at. And am I now (after all the vexation it has given me, to keep it so) to have my fair fame blown upon, and thawed, by the foul breath of your scandal?—Indeed, Master Steward, you are extremely wrong, to—"

"Very true, as you were going to say," interrupted old Lewis; "so I'll hear the rest of your *metaphor* another time. At present, my good Leonarda, take that poor babe, give it something to eat, and put it to bed."

During this altercation, Carlos had been employed in chafing the child's limbs, as he held it before the fire. Leonarda, still muttering objections, approached to take the babe; but, as he held it to her, she uttered a loud scream and began to shake, as with an ague-fit; while the infant frightened at the noise, twisted its little fingers in Carlos' hair, and seemed to sue for his protection.

"What the devil ails the woman?" exclaimed Lewis, who was, himself, scared by her cry. "Did you never see a baby, before?—Come, come, rouse yourself; take a glass of Malaga, and carry a flask to your own chamber."

It required little enforcement to bring Leonarda to obedience of this order; and at length she received the child, though with a very ill grace. Carlos observed this; and requesting her to be very careful of her charge, slipped a pistole into her hand. The bedlam's harsh features instantly relapsed into a complaisant smile; she dropped a curtesy, assured him, it should not be her fault if the child fared not well, and retired.

"Well," said Lewis, "now that your babe is taken care of, let us have some care for you."

Having assisted his guest to change his apparel, he placed a cold capon and a flask of excellent wine on the table, of which he earnestly pressed him to partake. The log, which Lewis' care had thrown on the fire, crackled loudly, diffusing a genial heat, and lively light, around; and Carlos could not but be grateful for the contrast of his late, and present, situation. Nevertheless, the local comfort which he now enjoyed, could not erase the sorrow which had taken deep root in his heart; retrospection brought full on *"his mind's eye,"* scenes which he would fain have banished from his memory; and repeated, but involuntary sighs burst from his breast.

"By Saint Iago, it moves me to see you thus," said his entertainer. "Take another glass; wine does wonders."

Carlos complied; but, in this instance the boasted virtue of the grape availed not.

"I would," rejoined the steward, "I had the power to drive away this plaguy melancholy! it should not trouble you long. Well, well, I do not wish to pry; but, I think I can guess the cause. Love, love, hey, Signor! is it not? By Saint Iago! I believe I am right!"

"I beseech you not to trifle with my feelings!" quoth

Carlos. "My wounds are too tender to admit the probe of ridicule—my sufferings too severe to be scoffed at."

"I never was much addicted to scoffing—particularly at the sufferings of any one—or to sport the produce of my own brain, at the expense of another's feelings," replied Lewis in a serious tone. "I ask your pardon, Signor! I saw you melancholy, and I wished, as far as in my poor power lay, to remove it. I pray you pardon me! I hoped to cheer you—but I will say no more."

To the accent of sympathy Carlos had been unused, and it sunk to his soul. He wished to entrust his entertainer with his story, as well as to claim his advice—which his venerable appearance bespoke him well-calculated to bestow. His furrowed cheeks (for Lewis had numbered seventy winters) his hoary locks, thinly scattered over his temples, and his dark eye, which though time had dimmed its lustre, would faintly sparkle at a merry story, or moisten at the tale of woe, insured all hearts, and won his guests' esteem.

"If, in this instance," thought Carlos, "the face be not an index to the mind, I am much deceived. Besides, what risk do I run, by my confidence? 'Tis most improbable my persecutor should seek me here." A sigh escaped him, at the remembrance of who that persecutor was; and—"I'll trust this hospitable creature—" was his resolve.

"Father," said he, "your hospitality demands more than my thanks. But, alas! such is my wayward lot, I can no other way evince my gratitude, than by unfolding my sad story; with the circumstances which drove me an alien from my native home. Oh! had I foreseen the destiny that awaited me, I had not, surely, lived to merit it!"

"Were the book of fate open to our view, few, haply none, would have philosophy to encounter the dark pages allotted them," observed Lewis. "But, by adding little and little, as we load beasts of burden, wonderful is the weight of misery which the human mind is capable of supporting. But, come, pledge me in a glass of Malaga, Signor; and then, if it please you, your story. If my advice, or aught else, can befriend you, you shall not lack it: if not, be satisfied, you shall never repent your confidence."

Carlos made answer, he entertained no doubt on that subject; and thus commenced his tale.

CHAP. II.

List a brief tale!
And when 'tis told, O that my heart would burst!

KING LEAR.[1]

"NOT many leagues distant from the city of Toledo, stands the mansion of my ancestors; a solitary castle, situated at the foot of a lofty hill, and shrouded in the deep gloom of an o'erhanging wood. No sound invades the silence; save where hoarsely roars the adjacent cataract, or when the moping owl hoots on the lofty battlements.

"In this sequestered spot, which seemed congenial with his disposition, my father past the greatest part of his time. Gloomy and impenetrable, he shunned society. The voice of mirth augmented his chagrin; while whole hours would he seclude himself from his family, and on his return, sit buried in reverie, nor utter a syllable to any one.

"I was reared at the castle, and hardly ever quitted it during my boyish days.—Days to me of sorrow!—The voice of parental tenderness never saluted my ear—never spoke pleasure to my heart; bitter taunts, often accompanied by blows, were my constant fare, and not a hope to sweeten it.

1 Shakespeare, *King Lear* (1605), 5.3.177-178.

"In this state of misery, I attained my eighteenth year: as I advanced towards manhood it became more intolerable; and I resolved to avail myself of the first opportunity that might offer, to escape from parents so unfeeling, and to dedicate my life to the service of my country.

"The anxiety of my mind impaired my health, and one night, unable to sleep, I left my bed, with an intention of wiling away an hour or two, by a ramble in the neighbour-ing wood—on the gloom of which I was wont to sit, and brood over my inquietude. As I crossed the vestibule, I was startled by the rattling of keys; and had hardly time to con-ceal myself behind a column, when a door opened, and my father stood before me. His countenance was haggard, his eyes shot a wild glare around, and he carried a dagger in his hand. He secured the lock, with a tremulous motion, and proceeded towards his own apartment.

"I was wrapt in astonishment, for the door whence he had issued, communicated with a ruinous priory, attached to the castle, and which was reported to be haunted. Many years it had been untenanted; and the portal, I have named, was supposed to have remained closed, during that period. No wonder therefore that my admiration was excessive, on seeing my father issue at dead night from such a place; his features distorted, and an instrument of death in his grasp.

"I tried the door, but it was fast locked; I then returned to my chamber, and throwing myself on the bed, I passed an almost restless night; and so much were my thoughts occupied by my father's late mysterious appearance, that even in my slumbers, they recurred to me.

"Towards dawn, I dropt into a slumber, when methought, having gained ingress to the priory, I wan-dered through the gloomy aisles, contemplating the sur-rounding emblems of mortality, till I came to the brink of a deep gulph, that obstructed my way—over which a rotten plank was laid, and appeared the only path by which I could reach the other side. With fear and caution I pursued my way; and had past about half over, when suddenly my father met me. Vengeance flashed from his inflamed eye-balls: he drew a poniard from his bosom, and stabbed me to the heart; then, with a horrid shout of exultation, that made the vaulted roof resound, he hurled me headlong down the yawning chasm! and shrieked—*"There die! and die the secret with you!"*—Oh! God! what were my sensations!—Methought I fell into a lake of blood; and the crimson fluid, which rushed in a torrent from my heart, seemed to increase the stream!—I struggled hard but was on the point of sinking—when a sound of heavenly music assailed my ravished ears; the scene of blood vanished, and a figure of angelic beauty, stretched forth a hand to raise me, and pointed to a path, enamelled with the rarest flowers, and margined with the choicest fruits of autumn. I gazed with rapture; when a ray of light, like the meridian glory of the sun, fell upon my dazzled eyes, and awoke me.

"My dream left a powerful impression behind: I longed to explore the mystery which I deemed adherent to the priory—but how to satiate my curiosity?—At length, I remembered a large bunch of keys, which hung neglected, in a room next my own; and trusting that some of them would answer my purpose, I fixed on that night for my attempt to visit the priory.

"Accordingly, when the clock struck twelve, I descended to the vestibule; and had just applied the first key, when the lock was turned from within, and ere I had well time to secrete myself, my father again appeared—the poniard in his hand, and the same ghastly look, as on the preceding night.

"He closed the portal and disappeared.

"I then renewed my attempt; I tried every key several times to no purpose; and was at last compelled to forego my design, and retired, sullen and disappointed, to spend a second restless night. For such was my anxiety, augmented by my late dream, to explore the interior of the abbey, that the desire became, as 'twere, a part of my existence.

"I rose early, and strolled into the garden; where I encountered the gardener, a domestic grown grey in service of the family. After some converse, I introduced the subject nearest my heart; thinking—from his long servitude—he might throw some light upon it, and amongst other questions, asked him, if he had ever been within the priory?

'The virgin forbid!' exclaimed the old man, in visible agitation. 'I would not enter those walls for the throne of our good King Ferdinand. I shudder at the very thought of it!' "Indeed!" cried I, hoping, if he were master of any circumstance that might alleviate my curiosity, to lead him to declare it. "Why so, honest Gulielmo?"

'Because, Signor,' replied he, 'though heaven be thanked! I am a good christian, I do not think myself a match for ghosts and hobgoblins.'

"Ridiculous!" said I. "I had a better opinion of your understanding, Gulielmo, than to suppose you the dupe of a superstitious report, calculated to scare a grandam, by a winter-night's fire."

'Then you don't *believe* in ghosts?' interrupted old Lewis.

Carlos smiled, and continued his tale thus: "This is more than report, Signor:" 'I remember the business as well as if it had happened only yesterday,' said the old gardener, as he leaned on his spade, and with a mournful look, gazed on the spires of the priory, which were visible above the garden-wall. 'Your grandfather lived in the castle at the time; and, as soon as he discovered the murder, swept the priory of the bloody-minded friars, who committed it. Ah! 'twas a most villainous deed!'

"Finding him so communicative, and entertaining hopes that I should glean from him whatever he knew, relative to the abbey, I told him I had often heard the story; but, with so many variations, and improbable, nay impossible events, that I should consider my understanding libelled, were I to say I credited it."

'As sure as there is a God above, the story is true!' said the old man, with solemnity. 'I remember the affair; and if you please you may take it from my lips, Signor.'

"Having given my assent, the old man rehearsed his tale, as nearly as my memory will serve me in these words:"

'You are to know, Signor, that the last prior of yonder place, was confessor to the convent of Saint Agatha, situated about a league to the northward of this. Among the rest, there was a nun, who (as I've heard) was as much handsomer than any of her sisterhood, as a carnation is before a wall-flower. On her, Father Anselmo cast an eye of desire; and, forgetting his vows, and losing the fear of God, he determined to seduce her. As he had a goodly person, was not an old man, and had (like the first tempter) a smooth tongue, he succeeded but too well; she listened to his persuasions, and became the victim of his desires. At length, fearful their intercourse might be known, he prevailed on her to leave the convent, and abscond with him to the priory—where she tarried in the disguise of a monk.

'After a time she became pregnant; which proved the cause of the bloody tragedy that followed. The idea of the business coming to light, filled him with dread (which always follows a bad action sooner or later) and turned his love to hatred. He forgot the pains he had taken to seduce her from the path of virtue; and even considered *her* as the cause of the mischief that might ensue. In this temper, the devil whispered in his ear, that there was *one* way, and a sure one, of burying the secret for ever: Again, the poor deluded wretch listened to his arch-deceiver; and to avoid the consequence of one sin, plunged into another of a much deeper dye.

'Under pretence of kindness, he prepared a posset for the poor nun; who had not long swallowed it, before she was seized with convulsions. Then did this devil, in human shape, shew his cloven foot, by deriding her pains, and insulting her with most unmanly jeers; and to conclude, exultingly informed her, he had mixed a poison in the posset she had just taken. On this, remorse for her past failing, her present pain, occasioned by the poison, and the terror of being thrust into the presence of her creator, with all her sins upon her head, caused her to rave most bitterly; so much that her screams reached my late lord, your grandfather, who was walking in the garden here. Her cries continuing, his lordship insisted on being let into the priory; which the monks refused, and even threatened him with an anathema, if he attempted it. He valued not their threats a real, but ordered his people to break open the gates: and, after some search, found the nun in one of the cells, in the agonies of death. My lord strove to comfort her; but, alas! she went out of this world, hopeless of the next!

'Just before her death, she informed my lord of these circumstances. Strict search was made after the murderer —who was at last found, suspended to a bar in his cell—a dreadful example of the divine vengeance, and another proof that no crime escapes eternal justice!

'My lord was so exasperated against the brotherhood (considering them all as abettors of the murder) that he made the affair known to the ecclesiastical court, and they expelled the priory; and, since then, the place has been shut up, and suffered to go to decay. Indeed, his lordship, on his deathbed (fearful he might have punished the innocent with the guilty) enjoined his successor, your father, to admit a new society, and left a considerable sum to that intent: but that did not suit our present lord's purpose; he kept it for—— Well well, no matter, I've done:—But I'll swear to the truth of what I have said; and, if the place is reported to be haunted, it is not altogether without foundation you see.'

"True," returned I; "but you broke off abruptly; you were about to say, my father kept the priory for some particular use—and you tell me it has (since the horrid transactions you have just related) been shut up, and suffered to decay. What is it you mean? your language is incomprehensible."

'Faith, Signor, I hardly know what I mean,' said the old man.—'It is of no consequence. Pray pardon me!—I have been idling my time in discourse—and must to work again.'

"Stay, Gulielmo," cried I. "That there is some secret, of which you are master, I am well persuaded—if so—"

'Secret, Signor! what secret should there be?' interrupted the old man, with evident trepidation.

"Come, come, Gulielmo, you were not born to dissemble," said I. "Impart to me, therefore, what you know, and rely on my secresy."

'Do not press me,' replied he, with increased agitation. 'It does not become a servant to criticise the actions of a master—much less, to lower a father in the opinion of his child.'—

"Spare your comments," interrupted I.—"Reveal what 'tis you know; I have reasons for wishing to be made acquainted with it, which you cannot be aware of. Proceed; I pledge my honor for my silence!"

'Then you are to know, Signor (Ah! the deeds of darkness are always brought to light, by some means!) that the wicked prior was not the only one, who, in that very building, was guilty of—'

"As the last word fell from his lips, a servant entered the walk we were in, and Gulielmo hurried away, spite of my efforts to retain him. The servant came to announce breakfast; and, very much chagrined, I followed him in. During our meal, which was, as usual, gloomy and unsocial, my mind reverted to its favourite theme; and, almost unconsciously, I inquired, what could be my father's motive for suffering the priory to continue in its present ruinous state?

"His emotion soon convinced me the question was a most unwelcome one; he cast a glance of fearful suspicion, and the confusion visible in my countenance, seemed to increase his. After a pause, he demanded my motive for the interrogatory. I replied, I conceived it might be repaired, at a very moderate expense, and rendered a comfortable asylum for a few holy men, whose prayers might atone the crimes that had been therein committed."

'What crimes?' demanded my father.

"Finding I had said more than it was my intention to have done, I made an hesitative answer, that all places upon earth were liable to be the scenes of vice—and that report went so far as to say, the priory was not an exception to the rule. He appeared as if struggling to make a reply; but, at length, boiling with anger, he burst from the room —muttering a curse upon me.

"He soon returned, saying it was his intention to depart for Toledo, immediately; and, the same day, we set out for that city, without my having an opportunity of any further conversation with Gulielmo.

"Our journey was unattended by any particular occurrence; and soon after our arrival, I was introduced at my father's table, to a lady, whom he called Donna Seraphina. It was with infinite difficulty I restrained my mirth, on her name being announced—for never I believe, was there one so ill-adapted to the bearer. Her face was round and unmeaning—her eyes goggle—her hair carotty—and her bulk enormous. I was somewhat surprised at the marked attention which both my father and mother paid her; the former particularly—as I had never before seen him so observant of the rules of politeness. This, however, was soon accounted for: on the lady's departure, my father was lavish in his panegyrics on her in which he was most ably joined by my mother, and their eulogiums ended in asking my opinion of her—but, in such a manner as gave me to understand they expected an implicit assent to theirs. I was not, however, hypocrite enough to disguise my senti-ments, but frankly told them the effect which the mention of her name had had upon me; and that as he appeared to be her friend, I thought it would be a friendly act to advise her to change it. He bit his lips, eyed me with anger, and told me that Donna Seraphina was a widow of immense fortune and amiable manners; that she had seen me on the day of my arrival at Toledo, and was so well pleased with my person (such were my father's words) as even to intend me the honour of making me her husband.

"I found it impossible to preserve my gravity, but burst into a fit of laughter.

'Fool!' exclaimed my father, 'know better than to treat a woman of her description with disrespect.'

"Far be it from me; age is too honourable to be treated with disrespect," quoth I. "But as the lady has deigned to confess a partiality for me, she may as well prove it by adopting as by marrying me; as it will be much pleasanter to me, and will better become the disparity of our years.

"With extreme asperity he said; 'I have listened to *you*—

now hear *me*. Donna Seraphina proffers you the honour of her hand, and my word is pledged for your acceptance of it. Either enable me to fulfil my promise, or take the consequence of your disobedient refusal. I will hear nothing you have to say—unless it be an unconditional acquiescence. Begone, Sir! and when you have learned the duty of a son, you will find in me a father.'

"I retired, not without some slight sensation of indignation, at what I thought, his abuse of paternal power. It was night, and thinking the streets best calculated for reflection, I went out.

"As I turned the corner of a narrow lane, I heard a shriek, as from a person whose mouth was muffled; and presently beheld two men wrapped in cloaks; bearing a woman in their arms. I commanded them to halt, and inform me whom it was they carried apparently against her will. Again the woman uttered a faint scream, and the men attempted to pass without deigning me an answer. I drew my sword, and swore, through my breast they should force a passage, unless they satisfied my inquiry; on which they both attacked me. I was so fortunate as to disarm one of them, who strove to regain his sword, but I stabbed him in the arm; and, by a sudden spring, tore the lady from the other ruffian, at the moment she fainted—and, throwing her across my shoulder, was thus obliged to sustain the combat—till I was wounded, and fell to the ground with the lady in my arms."

CHAP. III.

I swear to thee, by Cupid's strongest bow,
By his best arrow with the golden head,
By the simplicity of Venus' doves,
By that which knitteth souls and prospers love:
And by that fire which burn'd the Carthage queen,
When the false Trojan under sail was seen;
By all the vows that ever men have broke,
In number more than ever women spoke,
In that same place those hast appointed me,
To-morrow truly will I meet with thee!

A MIDSUMMER NIGHT'S DREAM.[1]

"Recovering," continued Carlos, "I found myself in a chamber, surrounded by strangers, and a lady beside the couch whereon I lay. Her exclamation of, 'Heaven be praised! he survives!' uttered in a tone sweeter than a Seraph's voice, attracted my attention: I looked up and beheld a face lovely beyond description, and which, time or misfortune can never erase from the tablet of my heart. I soon learned that she was the person in whose defence I had drawn my sword; for she began to pour forth her thanks in such a manner as might have made a coward doff his fears, and glory in the danger he might encounter for her sake. I also found, that at the moment I fell, the cavaliers (who were in the room) came up, and saved me from an untimely end. The lovely stranger, having repeated her acknowledgments, took her leave—with a wish breathed for my recovery, and a promise to visit me on the day fol-

1 Shakespeare, *A Midsummer Night's Dream* (published 1600), 1.1.169-178.

lowing—but not till she had presented me with a ring, as a token (so she was pleased to say) of her grateful esteem. She, then, departed; bearing with her an heart—which while it beats, will beat for her alone!

"I was confined many days to my bed, at the house whither I had been conveyed on receiving my hurt; and during that painful crisis, neither saw or heard from the lady; and the agitation of my mind, on that account, much retarded my recovery. When I was able to remove, I bade a grateful adieu to my host, and returned to my father's to whom I had written, during my confinement, without once hearing from or seeing him—and, on my arrival at home, he jeeringly said, he hoped my late chastisement would be a warning to me, not to trouble myself, in future, with things which did not concern me.

"This had little effect on me, so inured was I to my father's want of tenderness; but alas! I could not repel the unkindness as I thought it, of my fair unknown with the same indifference. Had I possessed kingdoms, I would have given them all to have ascertained the name and abode of my beloved. In this state of mind, I was accosted by a page, in the street, who having delivered me a letter, vanished in an instant. The billet was from a female, and this the purport of the contents.

"She regretted not having seen me since our first interview; but begged me to believe it was not any want of esteem, but the respect due to the opinion of the world, that had prevented her visiting me, during my illness. As a proof of the desire she had to cherish the acquaintance, if I would take the trouble to walk in a certain place, at a certain hour that evening, I should find a person who would give me every information I could wish.

"I kissed the paper a thousand times, and ardently longed for the close of day, which was to bring me to the presence of her I adored. At last, the wished-for hour arrived, and I walked, or rather flew to my appointment. I examined every female face that past me, but none bore the least resemblance to her I sought; and I threw myself on a bench in despair, when a lady (who had crossed me more than once) came and seated herself beside me.

"After two or three hems—'I find,' said she, 'you are punctual; the case too rarely with you cavaliers—who generally spurn from you the heart which acknowledges your masterdom.'

"Do me not such injustice," I cried, "nor weigh my love in the same balance with a common passion; it was a treason against the Deity."

'Indeed! may I believe you?' demanded she.

"By all the Saints you may!" I returned. "Did you know the mental agony I have sustained since my interview with the lovely writer of the lines which led me hither, you would no longer doubt me. Then haste and bring me to her."

'Behold her *here!*' cried she, in a languishing tone, and throwing back her veil; when the moon-beams falling on it, displayed to my astonished sight—a face round and inexpressible as the orb of night—in which I recognized the features of my old inamorata, Donna Seraphina!

"My surprise and disappointment rivetted me in silence to the spot; which the lady ascribing to my excessive joy, laid her hand on mine, and sought to encourage me by a full and verbal declaration of her passion. As soon as I recovered my power of speech, I interrupted her eloquence; requesting her not to take the trouble to repeat what it was incompatible with my honour to hear—avowed my affection for another—and was about to withdraw—perceiving my design, she caught hold of my cloak and began to play off all the airs of a slighted girl—which on a corpulent dame of sixty, sat very unseemly. This redoubled my disgust; I again interrupted her—repeated my heart was not my own—and wished her a good night. Then (Oh! never shall I forget it!) did she pour out a torrent of abuse upon me; protested my father should be made acquainted with my conduct, and with many bitter imprecations departed.

"I soon found she had been as good as her word; next day my father vainly endeavoured to smooth his brow, bade me hold myself in readiness to depart from Toledo on the following morning—when it was his intention to return to the castle.

"On the night of our arrival there, he informed me he had a secret to entrust me with, relative to the priory. 'You have,' continued he, 'been very particular in your inquiry about that place, and I am now determined to let your curiosity be satisfied.'

"Rest assured, your confidence shall not be abused," said I. "I call heaven to witness for secrecy! and if I violate my oath, may never-ending torments—"

'Hold!' interrupted my father. 'I ask no promise—I require no oath—I'll have a better surety for your silence.'

"Whatever you require on that score, I shall cheerfully submit to my father."

'It is enough,' said he. 'Follow me.'

"He took a lamp and led me down a flight of stairs; and then along a narrow passage, at the end of which was a massy iron door. He applied a large key to the lock, and with some difficulty wrenched it open; when the condense air that rushed from within caused me to retreat; but my father seized my arm—telling me we had but a little farther to proceed, and bade me take the lead. I obeyed—and on gaining the threshold, he gave me a blow behind, that hurled me down a flight of stairs—and in the same minute closed the door and turned the key upon me."

'There,' said he, in an exulting tone; 'there learn obedience to the will of a father—there curse your inquisitive folly, which prompted you to attempt to dive into the secrets of your parent! Fool! didst thou think thyself unnoticed? No, no; I have marked thee for some time. But no matter, listen and tremble at the punishment that is awarded thee!—Know wretch! never shalt thou repass this threshold!—Within this noisome dungeon which now encloses thee (where hope dares not to enter), even there thou art doomed to pine away thy youth: there shall old age overtake thee, ere thou hast past thy prime; unless grown desperate at your situation, you dash your phrensied head against the wall—and prematurely end a life of filial disobedience!—I leave you to your fate!'

"He closed the grating at these words, but Oh! God! in what a state of mind did he leave me!—It would be as vain to attempt a description of it as it would be to count the forest leaves. I paced my dungeon with a hurried step—I accused fate—execrated the hour I was born—and almost mediated putting a period to my wretched being, by the means my cruel father had suggested—when tripping against something above the surface of the earth, I fell —and caught a skeleton in my arms!—

"But hark!" continued Carlos, "the castle-clock strikes two! —I have already trespassed too much upon your patience."

'Well, well, 'tis late to be sure; so we'll to bed,' said Lewis—'But to-morrow good Signor, you must favour me with the rest of your story; which I must own is somewhat strange. However, cheer up—do not despair—providence is all-sufficient; and, or I am much deceived, you have many happy days to come—and that shortly. Come, Signor, one more glass, and then to bed;—fill a bumper.—May every honest man meet with a recompence for the frowns of fortune, and every rogue see his error in time, and amend it!"

CHAP. IV.

Thou art a soldier, 'tis said a good one;
And I ne'er yet, knew a rough, true soldier
Lack humanity.

COLMAN, THE YOUNGER.

LEWIS led Carlos through the great hall, and up a noble flight of stairs, at the summit of which they entered a spacious gallery—the wainscoat thickly adorned with portraits of the family of Henares. The old man opened a door at the extreme end, and ushered Carlos into an extensive room, hung with green velvet, where he told him he was to pass the night.

"I have given you this chamber, which I like better than any in the castle—for it was my young master's," said the old steward, with a heavy sigh. "Poor Don Torrismond! haply you have not now a roof to shelter you!—That is his portrait, (pointing to one of a youth) and as like him as one flask in my cellar is like another. Tell me Signor, was he not a comely stripling? What a noble statue!—how expressive his full dark eye!—By Saint Iago! he was the flower of Henares!—I never look at his likeness but it brings the rheum into my eyes—and fearful I should be contagious, I shall wish you a sound repose—and leave you. But once more let me conjure you to be of good cheer—for there is a joy in store for you, of which you have not a foresight.'

Lewis withdrew—and left Carlos contemplating the portrait which had been pointed out to him: the features were peculiarly interesting and expressive; and the sigh

24

with which the old man had uttered his name, gave him cause to think the original was unhappy. "We are all born to trouble as the sparks fly upwards!" said Carlos as he turned from the picture.

He left the lamp burning and retired to bed—when in a short time he found himself, from his late fatigue of body and anxiety of mind, extremely feverish, and it was long ere he sunk to sleep. At length he fell into an uneasy slumber, from which he was awakened by the drawing back of his curtains, and beheld a figure standing over him with a drawn sword. Carlos was not much influenced by fear —he sprung out at the opposite side of the bed; on which the figure made a precipitate retreat, and closing the door, the current of air extinguished the lamp which Carlos had snatched up. To pursue this midnight visitant in the dark, would he thought be temerity: he therefore secured the entrance, threw himself on the bed, and rivetted his eyes on the door; whereon the moon-beams peering through the ivy-mantled casements, cast a chequered light. In this situation he remained till fatigue overcame apprehension, and the hand of Morpheus closed his eyes.

The rays of the sun falling full on his face awoke him; and when he reflected on the occurrence of the night, he was inclined to believe it the effect of a feverish imagination or a mere dream; and under that impression, he determined not to mention the circumstance to Lewis—who at that minute walked into the room to say the family waited breakfast for him. Carlos descended with the steward; and begged to see his youthful charge, who had accompanied him to the castle, on the foregoing night—and who was a lovely boy. He again recommended him to Leonarda's care, and presented her with another pistole by way of encouragement—which she accepted with many thanks, and many promises.

Carlos then accompanied the steward to an apartment, where he was cordially welcomed by a cavalier of about the age of fifty; his face seemed furrowed by the hand of care, and even in the faint smile with which he saluted his guest, melancholy appeared predominant.

"We are much your debtors, Signor," said the cavalier (who was the owner of the castle, Antonio, Count of Henares) "and I regret I had not the pleasure to bid you welcome last night. Rodorigo, join your acknowledgments to mine."

On this, a tall young man with a hooked nose, a sallow complexion, and a lowering brow, came forward, and paid his compliments to Carlos; but, without that sincerity of manner which the Count had evinced.

"And why should not I be allowed to muster among you, in thanking this brave young stranger?" cried a third. "Is it because I have not got a battalion of smooth words to pour like grape-shot into his ears? Your hand, young man! receive the grasp of gratitude—and trust me, the words come not less warmly from the heart, because discharged in the blunt style of an old soldier."

This speech was delivered by a rough looking gigantic elderly man, in a scarlet doublet; with a patch over his left eye, and a marvellous well-turned leg——in *wood!*

Carlos was at a loss to account for the acknowledgments they so liberally poured forth—but was prevented requesting an explanation by a sight that rivetted him at the moment to the spot—and in the contemplation of which his every faculty was absorbed.

"Here," said the count, after a pause, "here is another, whose sense of obligation cannot be too warm; and who will not, I am certain, hesitate to express it."

Still Carlos continued gazing on that which had so powerfully attracted his interest—nor did he hear the Count, until the latter rejoined: "allow me to present you an old acquaintance."

Carlos now turned and beheld the living counterpart of that whereon his eyes had hung, in surprise and admiration—beheld the lady who he had rescued from the ruffians at Toledo—and whose image had never been absent from his thoughts. The lady too was as much surprised as himself: she had, it is true, heard that a stranger arrived on the preceding night; but Lewis (who knew the female mentioned in Carlos' narrative, to be the Count's niece, from the circumstance of the ring, &c.) had imposed silence on himself—as far as related to Carlos and his young mistress —and till she joined the party she was ignorant who the stranger was.

"Good heavens!" exclaimed the enraptured Carlos —"is it possible?—Am I so blest as once more to——." He recollected himself, and rejoined, he was happy to have the honour of seeing her again.

"I assure you," returned Aurora (so was the lady called) with the most engaging innocence—"I assure you I am sincerely rejoiced to have this opportunity of expressing my gratitude, and repeating the thanks which are your due."

"Indeed they are many," observed the Count.—"A most extraordinary circumstance, Signor. My niece has been seven years in the convent of Saint Clare for her education, and I dispatched my son to Toledo, for the purpose of conducting her hither. On the morning that she quitted the convent, Aurora went to pass the remainder of the day with a sister-boarder, who had at the same time taken leave of it. My son Rodorigo," (pointing to the young man) "waited on her at night to escort her to her lodging; in their way to which, they were attacked by two ruffians, who demanded the lady—this her cousin refused, and drew

—but overpowered by odds, was obliged to relinquish his wish of protecting her, and to retire."

"And glad enough to do so!" cried the old soldier.

"By your courage," added the Count, "she was rescued from the villains, and I shall be happy to make any return within my power."

"To be sure; reward this young volunteer, and then you'll do no more than your duty," said the soldier. "Not like some of our commanding officers, who before they go into battle, call their men their friends, their brothers, (damn all palaver!) and cry 'Each man shall share in the glory of the day!'—But when it is over, who takes the credit of it?—He does to be sure, four times out of five—and once away from camp, thinks no more of his *friends* and *brothers*, than if they were so many damaged cartridges. Mind, I don't say this is always the case: no, no—there are good and bad of all sorts.—I remember a skirmish I was in with the Moors, with my old friend, Don Morano, under whose command a detachment of us was out, on a foraging party; and we were returning to camp, pretty well laden, when we fell in with a troop of Moors, three times our number. Morano bade us fear nothing: we took him at his word, and drubbed 'em damnably. Well, our commander in chief, on our return, began to pepper our captain with compliments; but he bade him halt. 'Here, my Lord,' said he, pointing to his men, 'if you think I deserve thanks, pay them; here, this is the *substance*—I myself, am but the *shadow* of Morano. I would not brag; but, if ever there was hard fighting, it was on that day. The enemy's force was drawn up on a plain—their cavalry stationed—"

The Count knew that Don Hannibal (that was the soldier's name) if once permitted to get into the heat of the engagement, would not quit it, till he had gone through it again.—

"And thrice he fought his battles o'er,
"And thrice he slew the slain!"[1]

He therefore interrupted him; on which Don Hannibal cried, "Brother, brother, you'll never let me have my story out! There's not one of the family will now listen to me. —It was different once!—When Torrismond was at home, he would sit and hear me for whole hours—and as I related some gallant action, his young blood would fly into his cheeks, and his eyes would sparkle——"

"I beseech you, uncle," said Rodorigo, "not to pursue this subject; it hurts my dear father's feelings."

"I wish his feelings had been a little finer, heretofore; before he drove the poor lad from his house—who is now perhaps (but God forbid!) without a home!"

"For Heaven's sake have more compassion than to pursue this theme!" cried Signor Rodorigo. "You know, it wounds my father to the quick; and indeed the mention of a worthless son cannot be grateful to any parent."

"A what?" exclaimed the old man brandishing one of his crutches. "Worthless! Torrismond! Hark ye! with all his faults, he was worth a whole regiment of such brain-spinners as you yourself. 'Sblood! the lad had some metal in him. I can't allow a man credit for abstaining from what he has no passion for: a field-piece without fire is a harm-less thing enough; but clap a match to it, and—whiz!—it sweeps all before it!"

"Let *me* entreat you to desist!" said the Count, the tears starting in his eyes.

Don Hannibal, with another blessing on his absent

1 John Dryden (1631-1700), "Alexander's Feast" (1697). Palmer's quota-tion of Dryden here is actually a conflation of lines 67-68 from "Alexan-der's Feast." Dryden's original text reads as: "Fought all his battles o'er again, / And thrice he routed all his foes, and thrice he slew the slain."

favourite, declared he had done; but, that what he said was true. The conversation now turned into another channel: all were profuse in their civilities to Carlos, whom, spite of his opposition, they insisted should pass some time at Henares Castle.

On the family retiring to rest, agreeable to an appointment he had made—Carlos sought old Lewis in the kitchen; and after a friendly glass or two, thus recommenced his tale.

CHAP. V.

Alas! alas! is it not like, that I,
— — — — what with loathsome smells,
And shrieks, like mandrakes torn out of the earth,
That living mortals, hearing them, run mad—
Oh!—shall I not be so distraught,
(Environed with all these hideous fears)
And madly play with my forefather's joints?

ROMEO AND JULIET.[1]

"I TOLD you," said Carlos, "that, falling to the ground, I pressed a rotting skeleton in my arms; from which I shrunk with horror and disgust.—I paced my prison backward and forward, and encountered many objects, which I ascertained to be coffins; and reflecting on the situation of the passage which led me thither, I judged myself to be in the cemetery of the priory.

"Of this I was soon convinced. A flash of lightning broke through a fissure of the wall, in my dungeon, and displayed to my startled sight, the view of a charnel-house, filled with marrowless carcasses.

"In this mausoleum, entombed with the dead, I had remained some weeks, as I judged by the visits my father

---

1 Shakespeare, *Romeo and Juliet* (1597), 4.3.44-50.

made at the grate with my bread and water—and my health, as my spirits had long been, were fast decaying—when one night (for so I judged from my father having not long left me) I was awakened from a slumber, into which I had just fallen, by a faint noise at the far end of the vault: I started up, and presently heard a faint voice chanting an hymn; Seraphic strains could not exceed them, and the soft cadence, at the end, struck on my heart—inspiring me with a pleasing melancholy. I listened, in hopes the delightful sounds would be repeated; but I was disappointed—all was silent, save the echo of my own sighs.

"My father, at his next visit, *condescended* to ask me if my spirit were humbled, and whether I were now willing to espouse Donna Seraphina? In as few words as possible, I told him, though his barbarous treatment might destroy my life, my spirit was not to be affected; and that I would rather take an hyæna to my arms, than the antiquated piece of ignorance and coquetry to which he would doom me.

'Mighty well, Sir,' said he, with a most insulting coldness: 'a little more reflection may cause you to think otherwise, and you have no fear of interruption.—'Tis now midnight; and till this hour returns, farewel!'

"He closed the door and left me; his words, I own, but little affecting me. I hoped to hear the harmony which had before ravished my senses, and to that intent, I threw myself on a coffin, one of which (such was my fate!) was now become my wretched pallet; when methought I discerned a glimmering light, in a remote part of my dungeon. I rushed towards the spot, and found it was admitted through a crevice, on one side of my prison; which on inspection, I discovered to be occasioned by the giving way of the cement, between the stones. I applied my eye to the orifice, and caught a partial glimpse of a figure in white; who at the instant vanished, and again all was darkness.

"Gulielmo's story shot like lightning across my brain —and this supernatural appearance (for such my reason, debilitated by confinement, partly hailed it) was cherished by me as an auspicious omen. I considered that by means of the discovery I had made of the cavity in the wall (into which I struck my dagger, to enable me to find it again) I might perhaps regain my liberty. My heart bounded at the thought, with grateful joy, for I considered myself no longer deserted by Heaven; and the foul whispers of despair vanished before the dictates of religion—as the last mists of night disappear before the sun.

"I set to work in my attempt to remove the stones; but though I employed most of my hours at the task, (my dagger being my only tool of workmanship) a long period elapsed, ere I completed it. During that interval, my father as usual, brought me my miserable allowance; and though I had in the early part of my confinement, sought to move his compassion, his contemptuous manner of treating me forbade my persisting; and from the moment I entertained the hope of extricating myself, I disdained to sue to one who had treated me with such unnatural severity.

"Having, by dint of extreme labour, effected a cavity large enough to admit my body, I recommended myself to the Virgin, and (my dagger being broken by the arduous task), I seized an human bone, and quitted my dungeon —the scene of darkness and despair.

"I groped my way through several rooms and passages —and at last entered a place where the light of heaven once more blest my sight, through the painted windows of what I found to be the priory.

"It was the close of day, and here I resolved to tarry, till night should be pretty far advanced, and then, if possible, to fly the hated spot for ever. As I sauntered up and down the aisles, my attention was engaged by the beauty of a monument, which I stopped to examine—and to my astonishment beheld characters scratched on the wall, beneath which I decyphered to the following effect.

'Oh! thou! whosoe'er thou art, that may chance to trace these lines, if compassion inhabit thy bosom, if vengeance for another's wrongs can fire thy soul, withhold not a tear, nor fail to avenge the fate of the murdered.'—

"I was proceeding, but was prevented by the sound of footsteps—and turning from the inscription, my eyes rested on my father!—He started, and seemed about to retire—but, as if actuated by a second consideration, he came up, and accosted me with more apparent kindness than he had ever been wont to do.

'You have but anticipated me,' said he, 'in thus enlarging yourself—it was my intention to have liberated you this night. Come, follow me—and let every hostile and unpleasant thought be buried in oblivion. Donna Seraphina shall no more be named—and you shall receive a reward for what has passed, which you little expect. This night shall put an end to all your cares.'

"He took my hand and pressed it—then conducted me through the doors which I mentioned in the early part of my narrative, having seen him pass through, and so, to his study, where he left me—saying, he would return anon. I threw open the lattice and inhaled the evening breeze, which after my confinement, I enjoyed with double zest— the hoarse din of the waterfall, and the croaking of carrion birds, were, after the monotonous silence, in which I had been lately buried, musical to my ears.

"My father returned, accompanied by two domestics.

'I promised you,' said he, 'an unexpected reward—but it shall be one you richly merit. Seize him and follow me. Seize him!'

"My heart swelled to give to my tongue the utterance

of its dictates—this second piece of treachery rousing my resentment almost to a pitch of enthusiasm.

"Hold!" cried I, brandishing the bone I had fortunately brought from my dungeon.—"Mark my words and credit them! I swear, by all my hopes of happiness here and hereafter! the first who advances to lay hands on me, I'll cleave to the ground!—Observe me, Sir! I have suffered enough from captivity to know how to estimate the blessings of liberty—and in defence of that darling attribute will I exert the strength nature has given me. Therefore my lord, call off your myrmidons—or if you persist in your design, the blood that may be split, be on your head!

'Cowards!' exclaimed my father, observing the servants pause—'do you hesitate!—Instantly obey my order. What, would you have the parricide escape?—Know, he has attempted my life! Lay hands on him I say—and let us resign him to the rigour of the laws he has offended!'

"I was horror struck at this accusation—but I was obliged to exert myself as I observed the domestics preparing to obey their lord's command. I put myself on my defence, and levelled the first with the ground—on which my father and the other ran from the room, calling for help. My situation was critical, as I knew they would return with a force too potent for a single arm to cope with. In this exigence I had no recourse but flight—the lattice was open—I threw myself from it, and was hurrying through the garden, when a rustling among the leaves made me pause, and my heart bounded with apprehension. But, my fears were soon dispelled, a favourite dog, (who paraded the grounds, as a safeguard) approached me, crouched at my feet, licked my hand, and demonstrated every sign of regard in his power. "Alas!" said I, mentally, "can a brute evince that affection for me, which a parent denies." The idea was momentary: my present danger banished every other thought, and I again exerted my speed, nor halted till I had penetrated into the centre of the neighbouring wood. There I did not tarry long; but pursued my flight— without knowing whither I was about to go, or what was to be my future fate.

"I had been five days on my irksome journey, travelling at night, and secreting myself by day—when I was over-taken by the storm on this mountain, and but for your hospitality had been left exposed to its further fury. For that hospitality you have my thanks, and ever will retain my gratitude—and I hope, spite of the heavy fate which now bends me down, I shall yet have it in my power to prove that gratitude.

"Now tell me, father, if without cause I murmur at my fate, or execrate the hour that gave me being?"

"That your sufferings have been great I cannot deny," replied Lewis.—"But do not imagine yourself singular in that instance—there are others who smart as severely as yourself have done. Nay, would you believe that one in this castle, and that no less than the lord of it, is now writhing under one of the sharpest strokes of fortune?"

"Indeed!" said Carlos. "Then I must not repine. That he has cause for melancholy, gives me much concern—for, or I am much deceived, he is deserving every happiness this world can yield."

"You say but what he merits, in saying every thing good of him," quoth the old man, in ecstasy. "A blessing on thy heart for thy good thoughts!" Then after a pause, with a sigh, and shaking his head, he rejoined: "Who is exempt from woe?—Worth is no shield against the attack of mis-chance—the good and bad are alike, exposed to them. But, truly, Signor, you have reposed a confidence in me, which I will never abuse—and in return, I will intrust you with the cause of my poor lord's dejection."

CHAP. VI.

"Look here, upon this picture, and on this;
"The counterfeit presentment of two brothers."

HAMLET.[1]

"You are to know," said Lewis, "that the family of Henares is of very ancient date—being able to trace their progenitors as far back as the time of that illustrious French monarch, properly called *Charlemaigne*; in whose wars against the infidels that ravaged Europe, they particularly distinguished themselves.

"In the civil wars between that sanguinary and unnatural monster, Peter the Cruel—and his brother, Henry de Transtamere, it was the fortune of one of the family of Henares to save the life of the latter in battle. That prince, on ascending the throne of Castile, well rewarded him for the service he had performed—he loaded him with wealth, created him a grandée, and assigned him the empathetic words: '*Salvator Regis*,' as his motto—nor did he confine that distinction to the one on whom he bestowed it only; but ordained it as a perpetual honour to his descendants.

"The true Spanish pride, which is, I believe, proverbial in the mouths of our neighbours, was cherished by many of this house, who strove by noble and wealthy alliances, still further to aggrandize their family. Not so the last count: far from wishing to barter the felicity of his offspring, for the sake of riches and honours, the *real* happiness of his only child, my present lord, seemed the sole aim of his

---

1 Shakespeare, *Hamlet* (1603), 3.4.52-53.

existence. At an early age it was Don Antonio's lot to fall in love with the orphan-daughter of a cavalier, who had nobly fought for his king and country; but (as is the case in many other countries) he did not receive the reward due to his services, and died poor—leaving his child under the protection of an aunt, who had hardly wherewithal to support herself.

"In this situation Don Antonio first saw her.—The tears of a lovely woman always penetrate the heart of sensibility; and beauty never attracts so forcibly as in the garb of sorrow.—He beheld her with pity; which between the sexes, is often love's foster-mother. To be plain, he became deeply enamoured of her—gained a confession that the attachment was reciprocal—applied to the old Count for his sanction—and with his consent, made her his wife.

"This castle was the scene of merriment for many a day—and the Count seemed to vie with his son in love for the lady who repaid his attention with the most respectful tenderness. They had not been married many months, when their worthy father was seized with a putrid fever, of such a malignant sort, that, according to the prognostications of the physicians, his death was inevitable. My old lord heard his doom with the greatest composure—and seemed only anxious to console his children, who hung on his bed drowned in sorrow—from which they refused to move, though cautioned against the risk they ran from the contagion. Agreeable to the predictions of the doctors, the Count expired—having previously recommended his domestics to the care of his son and daughter—on whose heads he invoked a parental blessing. The latter was conveyed from the chamber of death by her fond husband —both striving to administer that comfort to the other, of which each stood in too much need.

"Her fatigue and agitation brought on the young Countess's labour (she being far advanced in her pregnancy) and the same hour which gave to the father's arms two babes, snatched from him the partner of his heart.

"It would be impossible to describe to you his lordship's grief—he continued many months in a state that alarmed his friends—who believed he would soon follow his lady. The constant sight of the pledges of their affection, however, appeared in some degree, to console him—and his storm of sorrow (if so I may be allowed to term it) lashed itself into a calm of melancholy, whence neither time or circumstances has had influence to rouse him.

"Meanwhile, the twins, who were both boys, were reared under their father's eye—the first being named Torrismond—the other Rodorigo. Never, I believe did nature take more pains to prove the versatility of her powers, than in forming the minds of those two youths —whose contrast of disposition was evinced in many circumstances during their boyish days. Torrismond was all life, thoughtlessness, and good humour—Rodorigo sedentary, studious, and reserved:—Torrismond scorned to exculpate himself from any youthful failing at the price of another—Rodorigo cared not at whose cost he cast the burden of censure from his own shoulders, and often found means to throw the blame due to himself upon his brother, whose warm and generous temper could not see the cunning practised against him. In short, Torrismond was formed to grace human nature—Rodorigo to dis——. But, no matter.

"I cannot, Signor, give you a stronger idea of the difference of their dispositions, than by relating a circumstance, which though trifling in itself, demonstrated the future bent of their dispositions.

"I was with them at the castle-gate (they being then about fourteen years old) when a blind beggar with his dog chanced to pass by. Having occasion to re-enter the house, I was about to do so, when the nature of their discourse made me pause, out of sight, to hear the result of it.

'I'll bet you a dollar,' said the artful Rodorigo, 'that you don't hit yon cur, at the distance we are now from him.'

'Done!' cried Torrismond—and without reflecting what he was about to do, took up a stone and threw it —but missed his aim, and unfortunately struck the old man upon the leg—who fell. No sooner did Torrismond see that, than he flew towards him, threw himself on the ground beside him, and tearing off his own scarf, began to bind up the beggar's wound. His brother, with great apathy, walked up to the spot, and asked what he meant by degrading himself so far as to be seen attending on a beggar.

'No, no,' replied the other, 'I shall not degrade myself by what I am now doing: the shame was in the cause, not the effect.'

'Pooh! pooh!' said Rodorigo, 'come along—if we stay here, some of the servants may see us, and we shall per-haps get very severely reprimanded by our father.'

'I should be sorry for that—but I would even incur his displeasure, rather than leave a fellow-creature (myself being the cause of his disaster) in this state.'

'Do as you please,' returned Rodorigo. 'For my part, I am determined to keep myself out of mischief, if I can; and wish you much good of your present employment.'

'Hold! surely you but jest,' cried his brother.—'Assist me to carry this poor creature to the castle, where he may have his wound dressed, and get some refreshment.'

'Not I indeed!' replied the other. 'It is not any thing new to him I dare say: he is only a beggar, and used to buffets —this is but another added to the number.'

'The more inhuman you, not to feel for him doubly.

But go your ways for a brute! we can do without you,'
exclaimed Torrismond.

'Brute in your teeth!' retorted Rodorigo. 'I shall leave
you to your vocation; nor run the risk of being implicated
in a business wherein I have no share.'

'Go—' said his brother—'I always took you for one,
who would fly from danger. Unfeeling coward.'

'It is a lie!' cried Rodorigo.

"Torrismond sprung from the ground like lightning,
and before I could reach the spot to interfere, (for till then
I did not shew myself) he struck his brother down. The
latter rose, his face besmeared with blood, and muttering
revenge, entered the castle: while the other youth (regard-
less of his threats) turned to me, and asked me to assist
him in conveying the wounded man into the house. I represented to him the anger of his father, should he become
acquainted with what had happened—and which he most
probably would, if the old man were taken into the castle.

'Be that at my own peril, for be the consequence what it
may, I cannot leave this poor old creature. Besides,' continued he, 'my father's anger seldom continues long—and he
will never blame me for shewing I am sorry to have done
an injury.'

"I was charmed to find he had so much feeling—and
together we conveyed the mendicant to one of the servant's rooms. Hardly had we dressed his hurts, put him to
bed, and given him a glass or two of wine (a sovereign
medicine—my service to you Signor!) before we were
ordered to attend the Count. We found him with his
younger son—and he severely rated Don Torrismond for
his conduct, in wounding the aged mendicant, and ill-treat-
ing his brother. The youth heard these accusations with
modesty, but firmness. He confessed himself culpable on
the first charge, but wished to justify himself on the other.

His brother had irritated him beyond endurance, he said: and if the chastisement he received were irksome to him, it would have been more praise-worthy to have resented it, on the spot, than to have made himself an idle prattler —by annoying his father's ears with a repetition of their squabble.

"Mark!" observed Lewis, "I do not mean to justify this assertion—far from it—nor would he in his cooler moments have done so—for on being reconciled to his brother, the tears of regret trickled down his cheeks, as he conjured his pardon for the blow he gave him. No—I merely mention it, to shew you that the warmth of his temper was the occasion of what follies he committed— and that reflection never failed to scourge him for them.

"His reply still further irritated my lord—who strictly enjoined me to confine him to his room. I would have spoke in his behalf—but his lordship very peremptorily bade me leave the chamber and obey his command—and (pointing to the door, as to enforce obedience) I retired with my charge.

'Lewis,' said the noble youth, on reaching his apartment, 'Lewis, you must do me a favor—'tis in your power and I am sure you will not refuse me. That unhappy wretch whose disaster I was wantonly, but not designedly, the occasion of, must be taken care of. Here is my purse,' (taking out his little stock) 'and give him this golden cross —I wish I had more for his sake!—But good Lewis! Beg his pardon for me and assure him I will endeavour to render myself worthy of it, by relieving every necessitous person I may hereafter see.'

"I caught hold of his hand and kissed it," continued Lewis—"and could almost have worshipped him. I took his presents—but with a design of using them very dif-ferently to his instructions. I blessed him as I quitted the room—and felt a sensation of delight in anticipating the triumph he would enjoy, when the Count was possessed of the truth, and of the duplicity of Rodorigo who, unconscious that I had witnessed the whole transaction, had I knew, fabricated a tale to the prejudice of his brother.

"Early next morning I went to his lordship's chamber— and having apologized for the liberty I was about to take, desired to be admitted as an evidence in Don Torrismond's favour.

'As his advocate, I should suppose, you mean to say,' returned the Count, drily—'for his offence is so black, little I fear can be adduced on evidence in his favour.'

"Excuse me my lord, if I presume to assert, that much may be said in extenuation of his fault," I replied. "I trust, my veracity is not doubted—and I call God to witness (I beg your lordship's pardon!) for the truth of what I shall recount!"

"Having the Count's permission, I briefly laid before him each circumstance with candour. During my recital he appeared much agitated: at the conclusion he ordered me to send his sons to him, and to wait without the door till he called me.

"I obeyed; and from my station could hear every word that passed. He began by recapitulating the fault of his elder son; and ended by repeating that his accuser was his brother —at the same time demanding to know what he had to urge in his behalf. Though the evidence of Rodorigo, as related by the Count, was far from truth (he having declared that he strove to prevent the stone being thrown) whereas he was the instigator of it, though slandered grossly, the generous-minded Torrismond scorned to retaliate upon his accuser.—He bowed to his father but answered not.

'\'Tis well,' rejoined the latter; 'I have one witness, whose evidence is necessary. Come in Lewis.'

"Rodorigo changed colour.

'I think,' added the Count, 'that you told me, you were present at the transaction which yesterday took place: 'tis therefore my firm command that you declare each tittle of it. So shall justice be rendered to the injured, and my resentment, as far as it will extend, fall upon the guilty. Speak, nor dread the resentment of any one.'

"I must confess (perhaps 'twas wrong) that I related the affair, without omitting a single item that might tell against Don Rodorigo. The father heard me out; then called on his younger son for his defence. The culprit seemed abashed —but striving to collect himself, was about to make a reply —when he was prevented by the Count.

'Hold!' cried he; 'nor aggravate your offence, by attempting to defend it. I shudder at your extreme duplicity! Lead the unthinking into error, and then betray them? —Hence from my sight!'

'Oh! my dear father!' cried Torrismond, 'be not too harsh, (pardon my words!) Rodorigo did not injure me with design. I was the offender—the first offender—for I struck him. Ah! my dear brother, do not regard me so disdainfully!—I have erred in lifting my hand against you: but pardon that—as I do whatever your momentary resentment urged you to say against me.'

'Enough,' cried the Count, after a visible struggle with himself, 'if you forgive him, I must pardon him too—and may you as easily forget the wrong he has aimed to do you, as I much fear he will forget your clemency.'

"Don Torrismond threw himself into the arms of his brother, and wept upon his shoulder—while the other received his caresses with a freezing coldness.

"When the young noblemen attained their nineteenth year, my lord removed his family to Burgos, for the purpose of introducing them to the king and queen; and even on that occasion, they evinced traits of their opposite temper.

"The queen demanded of Don Torrismond, what he designed to make his future pursuit; to which he replied: 'the profession of arms, so please you, Madam.—While your Majesties have so many foes to cope withal, my only pursuit will be to diminish their numbers, and lower their pride; and I shall willingly spill the last drop of blood in your service.'

"The same question being put to Rodorigo, he made answer, 'that his family was indebted to the royal family for every thing; and that he should pursue whatever course might seem best to their Majesties.

"For once however, the wary Don overshot his mark: the queen displeased as I take it with the indifference of so young a man, as to his future pursuits, took no further notice of him; but the next day she presented his brother with a commission in her own guards.

"Well, Signor, Don Torrismond with all the fervour of youth launched into every folly and dissipation of the court: he gamed deep, was famed for intrigue, would frequently stay out all night—or if he returned, was generally in a state of ebriety.

"He continued in this irregular course, spite of the admonitions and censures of the Count; with whom Signor Rodorigo was playing a deep under-hand game, by adhering closely to his society, and losing no opportunity to poison his mind against his dissipated son.

"Things had been in this situation some months, and my lord had signified his intention of returning to the castle, when his cabinet was found broke open, and property to a large amount taken thence. The domestics were summoned and interrogated—but nothing appeared to criminate either of them, and they were dismissed. I remained with my lord, endeavouring to console him for the loss he had sustained; not in the intrinsic value; but in the picture of his late and still adored lady.—At this juncture Don Rodorigo entered the room, and was told what had occurred. He shook his head, sighed, and presented a letter to the Count; it was from his eldest son, and ran to this effect: He confessed the folly of his many past actions; and his regret that he had not seen them in due time for reformation, ere they hurried him into the commission of one—compared to which the rest were pure as snow. He continued, that his mind was ill-calculated to enter into explanations; which ungrateful task his brother had kindly undertaken for him. He conjured his father to allow for the provocation which had spurred him on to a crime, which would imbitter his days to come, and drive him an outcast from his family, unless he was so blest as to obtain his parent's pardon; and concluded, by suing for a blessing as well as forgiveness '*for the wretched Torrismond!*'

"The Count, in a faltering voice, desired Don Rodorigo to explain the meaning of this ambiguous epistle—which was at first refused—the fear of wounding a parent's feelings, *as he said*, restrained him. My lord however persisted—and his son with much seeming (I was going to say feigned) reluctance, declared, that the crime at which Don Torrismond glanced, was the robbery of the cabinet.

'Unhappy boy! he is doomed to shorten my days,' quoth my lord. 'But he is my son, and I cannot refuse him my forgiveness: I will write immediately and tell him as much.'

'Hold, my father!' cried the unnatural brother.—'let not your affection hurry you into a piece of false compassion, for which you may have reason to blame yourself. How many have drained the chalice of debauchery, and been reclaimed by sufferings?—The corporeal agony attendant on excess, is an indication of the divine will. Consider my father, if for a time you give him up to misery and remorse, reflection may return to him, and he may prove a blessing to your age: but if the school of adversity do not reclaim him, he is incorrigible, and not worth your further care.'

'Not worth my care?' repeated Don Antonio. 'Ah! Rodorigo! you may one day be a father!—But, as you say, it may be for his good—and I will write what prudence exacts, not what my heart dictates.'

'One word more, dear father,' said Rodorigo. 'An angry word from you would wound his heart—besides, you are very much affected, and unfit to write on such a subject. Let me address a letter to him then.'

'Do so, my son,' replied the Count: 'but tell him he has my forgiveness—I cannot withhold it from him.—Write to him, but do not drive him to despair—tell him that I have shed tears of blood—but do not drive him to despair.'

"Rodorigo inquired, if he should not, in his father's name, and as a temporary punishment, forbid him the house?

"The good old Count sobbing, as though his heavy heart would have broke, besought Rodorigo to say nothing harsh—but to write to his brother, and assure him, all that was past should be forgotten—upon a promise of future amendment.

"The day after, a beautiful girl, in deep distress, requested to see the Count. She was ushered into his presence—where she fell on her knees, and besought him to do her justice—declaring, that she had been seduced by his son Torrismond, under a solemn promise of marriage—and that her unhappy failing had hurried a beloved mother to an untimely grave. She recapitulated a number of arts, practised by her undoer, and seemed so full of grief, that my lord (promising to provide for her) in the heat of anger, cursed his unhappy son!

"Pardon me!" continued Lewis, drawing the back of his hand across his eyes—"'tis an unpleasant theme to dwell upon.——I loved my young master as dearly as if he had been my own son—and would have given my life to—Pshaw! I am wandering!

"Well, from that hour no intelligence reached us—nor has my honoured lord since that fatal time held up his head.

"Don Hannibal de Langara, the old officer, whom you saw, is brother to my late lady—and has raised himself by dint of merit, to the first rank in the army, to which his mutilated figure alone, will tell you he has a claim. His love for Don Torrismond was so great, that on his account, he detests the sight of Signor Rodorigo—whom, like myself, he considers the source of his brother's disgrace and flight. —These sentiments, which he seeks not to conceal, are the cause of many an unhappy minute to my worthy lord —who, I firmly believe, looks forward to the grave, as the wayworn traveller eyes the goal of his weary journey.

CHAP. VII.

Our court you know is haunted
With a refined traveller of Spain.
LOVE'S LABOUR'S LOST.[1]

If thou dost love, pronounce it faithfully!
Or, if thou think I am too quickly won,
I'll frown and be perverse, and say thee nay,
So thou wilt woo—but else not for the world.
ROMEO AND JULIET.[2]

CARLOS had sojourned at the castle about a month, when a lady was introduced to him, by the title of Marchioness of Valencia. She was a woman of a tall commanding figure, and possessed features strictly handsome—but she wanted that delicate softness of expression, which we think constitutes true feminine beauty—and which, joined to an *hauteur* of manner, quickly diminished the effect, which the first view of her charms was likely to occasion.

Philippa, Marchioness of Valencia, was the daughter of a nobleman, who being left a widower, took a second wife at an age when such a step was very unlikely to increase his domestic happiness—he being on the verge of sixty, and his bride elect not more than half that age. The result was what might naturally be expected; she ruled him with an iron rod, and extended her tyranny to all who were so unfortunate as to be under her dominion.

Little Philippa, then a child, was one of the objects of

1 Shakespeare, *Love's Labour Lost* (1598), 1.1.160-161.
2 2.1.136-139.

48

her persecution. In vain she appealed to her father for redress; and she had groaned for years, under the controul of her step-mother, when death kindly laid his icy hand upon her, and snatched her away to another world, whither her husband himself soon followed her.

Left her own mistress at an early age, Philippa acted the part of her deceased mother-in-law, and revenged herself for the tyranny she had endured, on the domestics and all who were subservient to her.

Being heiress to an immense fortune, she had a long train of suitors, from among whom, she selected a worthy and accomplished nobleman—the Marquis of Valencia. The voice of fame was very busy with her character (whether justly or not, the sequel will determine) and her husband not being of a temper to relish the reports, severely reprimanded her—and they lived for five years in a state of discord, when the Marquis was seized with convulsions, which deprived him of existence.

His widow mourned with all due ceremony: she admitted only select company, wore the deepest (but most becoming) weeds, and was not seen to laugh by any— whom she did not wish should see her laugh.

The time prescribed (*by custom*) for mourning the death of a husband, being expired, Philippa threw off her sable habiliments, and went to reside with the Count her relative at the castle of Henares—and there she had remained from that period to the time she was introduced to Carlos —who had heard of, but not seen her till now, since his arrival—she having been confined to her chamber, by indisposition. Rumour went so far to say there was a certain magnet at Henares, in the form of her cousin, Rodorigo, which attracted her—but the world is censorious, and time will prove how true or otherwise the assertion was.

Some few days augmented the society at the castle in

the persons of a young cavalier, named Hilario de Hara, his sister Agnes, and a half-witted coxcomical cowardly cousin called Buzzardo.

"Heigho!" cried the last, throwing himself into a chair, "travelling's cursed troublesome—the devil—I'm half dead!"

"By heaven! it's quite intolerable to hear you complain of fatigue!" said Hilario. "Here is my sister who rode with us, does not murmur at the exertion; and you—"

"No rule. Wonder people like exertion—would never move at all, could I help it—monstrous troublesome."

"Ridiculous!" cried Agnes; "we have hardly come three leagues, since yesterday-evening (for you know you would stop half way, *to break the neck of the journey*) and I am sure that can't have occasioned you any great fatigue.—But (turning to the circle) how do you do good folks!—Your donnaship—your ladyship—your lordship—and your generalship?"

"Well said, madcap!" cried Hannibal; "thou shouldst have been a man—for thou wouldst have made a proper soldier."

"How do you know?" demanded Agnes, "but on an emergency I could head a troop of my own sex, and march to the right, or wheel to the left, as well as any veteran among ye?"

"We do not doubt it," replied Antonio. "But pray inform us how you have left all at the castle of Hara."

"All that *are* left are well," cried Hilario, laughing. "My old aunt, as usual, strumming on her crazy guitar—the portraits of my ancestors enveloped in dust—the furniture decaying—and the mansion itself falling, in compliment to its neighbours (the trees) which I have taken the liberty of removing. All gone! and what's worse, the money they fetched gone too, egad!"

"Prithee, stand still, and keep your sword from my legs!" cried Buzzardo; "it is troublesome."

"That is what my enemies say," retorted Hilario.

"Hate enemies," rejoined the fop—"troublesome too —trouble's my antipathy."

"And what do you call trouble?" cried Don Hannibal, in a voice like Stentor's—and which (the old commander being seated next to him) for once at least, roused Buzzardo from his *ennui*, and made him start from his chair. "You talk of trouble!—what would your dainty worship say, if you were in camp, and heard the drums beat to arms, before you were well in your first sleep?—How should you like to be sent on the forlorn hope, or march for four and twenty hours, knee-deep in water?—What would you say when you came into battle, and heard the shot and arrows whistle round you, like hailstones?"—

"Can't tell—never tried."

"I wish I had an opportunity of shewing you a sample!" exclaimed Hannibal. "I'd give you a billet on the other world with fright.—I remember, we had such another flimsy piece of camp-equipage when I was a younker in the army. We were close, besieged in a small garrison-town (I forget the name) near Granada; and this spark's greatest affliction was, that he could not get a reinforcement of wash-balls! However, he was not altogether disappointed; for they gave us such a volley of balls, of one sort, as were too hard of digestion for some of us.—It was day-break, in the month of May, when the Moors began the attack with such a shower of—".

"Apropos!" interrupted the Count, willing to avoid the heat of the engagement, into which he saw Don Hannibal about to dash, "I have been honoured with a letter from my sovereign—requiring what aid I can send him to prosecute the war, which he is resolved to wage against the treacherous Moors, for having broken the late treaty. And so, those youths who prize their fame above their lives, have now a glorious opportunity to distinguish themselves, under the immediate eye of their monarch.

Carlos could not conceal his transport—but with exultation, professed his intention of joining the standard of King Ferdinand, as a volunteer. Rodorigo declared the same resolve, but was opposed by the Count.

"No my boy, thou must not quit me," said he, "should the hand of ruthless war lay thee low—my sole-remaining prop! I have no other son to recompence me for thy loss, or close my dying eyes. But, though parental tenderness restrains thy ardour, my king shall not find the house of Henares slack in duty—for I will equip an hundred men, who at my own cost shall be maintained. Carlos shall lead them to the royal camp; and with the letters I shall give him, will be received as my proper son. Soon as the complement can be raised, he shall depart; nor do I know that man (and let me not be thought to flatter) in whose custody I would more readily deposit my honour."

Carlos bowed, and laid his hand upon his heart, for that was too full to find immediate vent for words; but though his tongue was silent, his eyes spoke the workings of his soul. At length, his cheeks flushed with grateful exultation, he replied:

"Words would be inadequate to express my feelings; but by endeavouring to merit the distinguished name of soldier. I shall hope to prove myself not unworthy of your lordship's favor, or forget the vast debt which you have heaped upon me."

"Well said, my brave boy!" cried old Hannibal; "I'll be your hostage that you make a good one. I would with all my heart, I were some twenty years younger! you should not go to the field without a comrade. It would not be the first time I had made those dingy dogs dance to the music of their own cries. Now, time has stolen a march upon me, and I should be of no more use in the field, than an unstrung bow, or a piece of spiked cannon; but I remember when I could have stood a brush with the stoutest; and the first day I smelt powder, was such a day as would have spoiled a squeamish stomach for fighting. The enemy were posed in a narrow defile, with a morass in their front —through which we waded, and coming upon 'em sword in hand, we did dust their swarthy jackets for 'em to be sure. The black battalions ran and screamed, that you would have thought it had been a holiday in hell, and that all the devils had broke loose to keep it!"

So ended the conversation, part of which had made a deep impression on the mind of Carlos.

Delighted with the pleasing prospect, which hope pictured in the blowing colours of youth, he that evening wandered over the mountain; whence in his present state of mind, he observed a thousand till now undiscovered beauties—and as he eyed the hospitable castle, his bosom swelled with gratitude to Providence, and to the Count, for the revolution in his circumstances. When first he entered beneath that roof, he was an outcast, forlorn and hopeless—now, his fortunes seemed to blossom—for he was about to hold a situation he had most coveted, and should henceforth eat the luxurious meal of independence, earned by his sword.—Still his felicity was not perfect—one thought served to allay his state of happiness —that was love. From his first interview with Aurora, he acknowledged the power of that Deity—and the more he saw of her, the more was he persuaded his fetters were rivetted for life.

He had just reached the angle of a rock, when a voice, which he recognized for that of his mistress struck his ear:

her person was not visible, but he heard her deliver herself to this effect.

"Tarry wanderer!" said she—"wither would you stray? —Ah! ingrate! thou art too like mankind, and wouldst fly the arms that seek to shelter thee.—Alas! thou art not the only one who would leave me to mourn his absence!"

Whether it was that Carlos felt a pang of jealousy, but the blood rushed to his cheeks, and he cautiously advanced so as to have a view of Aurora without being seen himself. She was seated near the base of one rock, and on the summit of another, her back was towards him—and she was caressing a lamb, who was endeavouring to extricate himself from the bondage of a ribband, by which he was retained.

"Unkind one!" continued Aurora, "is it in vain I wish to keep thee with me—thou wouldst begone—perhaps, for ever!"

As she concluded, the animal by a sudden spring, snatched the ribband from her hand—and bounding away, incautiously fell from the precipice, near which his lovely keeper sat; who started up, exclaiming:

"Oh! Heaven! my poor Carlos! thou wilt be killed!"

Here Carlos darted from his concealment, and speeding towards the spot:

"Fear not lady!" said he; "I will recover your little favour-ite, or perish in the attempt."

"Oh! say not so!" cried Aurora, with tender anxiety—"you could deprive me of nothing that I value half so much."

These words from the lips which uttered them, would have inspired Carlos to undertake impracticabilities: he darted down the precipice like an arrow, and quickly brought the runaway to its mistress; who returned her thanks with an embarrassed air, an hesitative voice, and cheeks flushed with blushes.

"I beseech you not to mention thanks, where they are

so little deserving," said he, "if my poor service merit aught, the remembrance of your feeling declaration will trebly overpay me."

Her blushes increased to a crimson hue, as she flattering, replied:

"Could I, when I saw you hazarding your existence for my gratification, think much to acknowledge your life was of more consequence than that of this little wretch, whom you have brought back to me? Oh! no; my heart is not so callous as to insensible of what it owes you, on more than one account."

"Beauteous Aurora!" cried the enraptured Carlos —"lovely in mind as in person! These words would compensate an age of torture; for to merit a place in your esteem is the proudest aim of my ambition. Ere long, I quit the sheltering roof of your noble uncle, for the clangour of arms, and all the perils of the field. Yet, wheresoever my duty may impel me—e'en in the ghastliest scenes of death—your image will be present to me—will fire me with a double thirst for glory—and in the last agonies of departing breath, 'twill be a consolation to think you take an interest in my fate, and will perhaps drop a tear to my remembrance."

"Alas!" rejoined Aurora, visibly agitated, "can I think of the wounds you received in my behalf? can I remember when pale and breathless you lay—your blood fast trickling—which had been shed for me. Can I—I say, reflect on this, and refuse you my gratitude—my esteem—my——? —Oh! you do not know my heart!"

"That I have your esteem, is more than I once dared hope to obtain. But, oh! how cold a return is it for that fervent, but pure sentiment, with which my bosom glows for you?" cried Carlos. "Yes, charming Aurora! I can no longer bury a passion that is interwoven with my existence. I love you!—to distraction love you!—I am sensible of my folly—but cannot resist it.—Oh! love! love! well art thou called a tyrant! since thou canst force to obey thy impulse. Pass but a little, I shall remove this form, where I can never more repeat this rashness; then do not, oh! do not kill me with your frowns—but pity and forgive me!"

"I know not how to answer you," quoth the maid, her eyes fixed on the ground. "By what I've heard, the strict punctilio subscribed to my sex demands that I should express resentment at your declaration; but I have still to learn what pleasure can arise from disguising our sentiments, and wounding the heart which professes we are dear to it. Know (and oh! Carlos! do not think worse of me, that I reveal it to you!) your passion is not unrequited. If your professions are sincere, I'll strive to merit them: if not, you will but have the triumph of laughing at, and I the mortification of repenting my credulity."

"Torture me not with the bare surmise!" exclaimed Carlos. "By every attribute, divine and human, I swear to the sincerity of my avowal! and that nor time, nor place, nor aught in possibility, shall ever make me waver!"

"Then, in return, hear me," said Aurora. "I call each power to witness this, my vow! that thou, and thou alone (as thou wert the first) shalt be the only master of my heart; and if our destinies deny my hand to you, it never shall be given to another!"

Carlos fell at her feet, carried her hand to his lips, and imprinted a kiss thereon, as a seal to his oath of constancy. Then, the evening being far advanced, he led her homeward—his spirits exhilarated to a degree, that none but the votaries of love can conceive, and none but the votaries of love express. Ere they reached the castle, Carlos obtained a promise from Aurora, that she would take his little protegée under her immediate protection, during his absence;

and the following day was fixed by them, for the baptism of the child, who was to be called Antonio, in compliment to the Count. The ceremony took place at the appointed time; Aurora and Carlos answering for the infant.

"Where have you been good people?" demanded Agnes, on their entering the castle, "surely you are wrong to risk health thus, in the evening dews: but, you have got a charming colour Aurora, you look ten thousand roses —and, were your love to see you now, he would bow to your charms with double devotion."

Aurora related the incident of the loss of her lamb; and that she was indebted to Carlos for the recovering of it.

"Don Carlos is peculiarly fortunate in having opportunities to serve you, cousin—and I dare say, you cherish the remembrance of his favours," observed Rodorigo, with something of a sneer. Aurora felt it; and with a degree of unusual acrimony, replied:

"I am sure, the amiable feelings which actuate Don Rodorigo, will never reprehend the dictates of gratitude. But I am more obliged to Don Carlos than you are aware of; for in the pursuit, he leaped an height that endangered his life—and I believe cousin it is not every man who will risk so valuable a consideration, on a woman's account— though she herself were in peril."

The allusion was to the time when Rodorigo left his cousin to the mercy of the ruffians, at Toledo, from whom she was rescued by the valour of Carlos: the first comprehended her meaning, and inwardly swore revenge.

"I saw you rush down the mountain like an hawk on his prey," quoth Hilario, addressing himself to Carlos.

"I saw you too," said Buzzardo. "Would not have done it for the world."

"You don't know what you would have done, had you been in my situation," observed Carlos.

"Know what I would *not* have done—what you did. Danger of hurting oneself; cursed trouble of climbing out again. Could not do it—heigho!"

The report of a carbine called the attention of the company; and, ere they could marvel at the cause, the explosion was repeated.

"Diabalo!" exclaimed Don Hannibal, "are we besieged —or what the devil is the matter?—I am too old and disabled, to turn out on the expedition: but, to the right-about, and quick march, youngsters!"

Rodorigo, Carlos, and Hilario obeyed; and Buzzardo in endeavouring to slink into a corner (for it would have been *troublesome* to have joined them) fell backwards, over the artificial leg of Don Hannibal, and threw down a flask of wine, that stood on a table near him; the purple fluid of which was visible on the chop-fallen countenance of the prostrate don; whose alarm was not abated by the vociferous curses of the old general—who swore he would have such a fellow drummed out of society.

Carlos and his companions now returned, supporting a cavalier, who wore the order of Calatrava, and whose clothes were stained with blood. Every means was used to restore animation, and the stranger at length opened his eyes; when, seeing himself surrounded by unknown persons, he faintly entreated pardon for the trouble he gave them. They begged him to be silent on that subject, and to command whatever the castle afforded, as though it were his own.

"I thank you," returned the stranger. "But where is my follower—my faithful Murdoch?"

"Here, your honour—here's little Murdoch Mc. Clud-derough," cried a voice like thunder; and at the same instant, the speaker thrust his head between those of Aurora and Agnes (who were anxiously gazing on the wounded stranger) to the no small alarm of both.

Little Mc. Cludderough was somewhat under seven feet in stature; with athletic limbs, a bushy head of carroty hair, and a countenance which would have kept any nursery in awe—where the name of *Buggaboo* had any weight—or expelled the crows to the distance of a league from where it was seen.

"You are not hurt, I hope?" said the cavalier.

"Hurt?" returned Murdoch. "Och! your honour, sure it's yourself that's hurt, and not me; and if you were not wounded, poor Murdoch would not be hurt, at all, at all!"

"My good fellow!" said the stranger—"I shall ever remember the brave manner in which you fought in my defence."

"Not a *syllabub* on that subject, my lord: or if you remember it, remember to forget it, if you *plaise*. Would not I have made myself second, or third to any dirty *spawl-pane*, if I had seen him overmatched?—But Saint Patrick protect you! you turn every colour in the rainbow; and you look as if you were dropping off the perch. Do, Signor Dons, for the love of charity! help my master to bed.—He's as well born as yourselves. And do you ladies put your fair hands to the business for him;—for he is an Irishman, and won't let your pains be thrown away. Or, if he should, his father, the Earl of Leinster will make you amends;—and if they should both fail, Murdoch will pay the debt for them, and himself too."

"We look for no reward, but the pleasure we shall derive in assisting him," said the Count. "But come; let us conduct him to bed."

"Och! Signor, why were you not born in little Ireland?" cried Murdoch. "But I hope your honour will be shortly served as my poor master, Lord Liffey has been; that Murdoch may have an opportunity to shew you an Irishman's heart is very unlike his head!"

CHAP. VIII.

This fellow is wise enough to play the fool.

TWELFTH NIGHT.[1]

LORD LIFFEY's wound had been given by a banditti, who made off, on the appearance of Rodorigo and his party; it was in a fleshy part of his ribs, and pronounced not dangerous; but the heat of the climate, the unskilfulness of the surgeon, and his own impatience, produced a fever, that confined him to his bed.

One evening, he was awakened by a violent noise in his room (not much unlike what may be conceived to be produced by the dancing of an elephant) when, throwing open the curtains, he espied his servant capering about the room like a dancing bear, with his head in a blaze. After many endeavours to extinguish the flame, Murdoch at last succeeded and his master demanded what had been the matter?

"Och! matter enough, your honor," cried Murdoch, mournfully, and rubbing his locks; "I've singed my poor pate, 'till there is no more hair upon it, I suppose, than a plucked capon, or a scalded pig."

"And how came it?" enquired Lord Liffey.

"As natural as life," returned Mc. Cludderough, whose good humour was seldom rustled but for a moment. "I ran my head into the candle, and strange as it may appear, my lord, it caught fire; and I would not be surprised (for a story

---

1 Shakespeare, *Twelfth Night* (1602), 3.1.53.

never loses in the telling) if it was to be reported that poor Murdoch is *light-headed!*"

"No, no—don't let that apprehension give you any uneasiness," said his master; "'tis a charge that can never be justly brought against you, or any of your family."

"There's no accounting for what people will say my lord: true or false, it must be authentic. But that is not the worst: a pretty figure I have made of my *knowledge-box*, by means of this *confloggeration* that, by my soul, if any body were to fall down and worship it, they would commit no sin against the scripture; for the devil a human thing it's like—except an *ould* bald-headed monkey, that a show-man brought to Kilkenny. I, that used to have the girls pulling caps about my most beautiful hair—so scarlet and bushy!—One saying: *Dear Mr. Murdoch! give me a lock, to make a lace to my boddice.*—For my lord, it was both long and strong, before I docked it a little (by cropping it close) to follow you to the wars.—And another crying—*Sweet Mr. Mc. Cludderough! give me one too, as a token.*" Och! they were devils for wanting the token!—To be sure, it is the fortune of war, as we say in French; but indeed Mr. Murdoch Mc. Cludderough, if Miss Judy Whacksonsterem was to see you, now your hopes would fly away like a great big whiff of *baccy.*"

"I believe your head is turned!" cried his master.

"By J——! I wish it was!—the wrong side before, that when I walked up to the glass I would not see myself."

"If you have one particle of common sense in your composition, leave this rhodomontade, and explain by what means you met with your accident."

"I did not meet with it, it overtook me; and I will tell you how my lord, in less time than you can cry—whack!" quoth Murdoch, endeavouring to soften his voice, and with a grin, which he designed for a smile.

"You must know, while your honour was taking your nap, as the pigs in my father's cabin do, and snoring like the beautiful drone of the union-pipes, (much good may it do you!) I thought I could do nothing worse than to do nothing at all; so I have been decyphering a small bit of a packet for my honourable mother, and my dutiful father, who bore me. Will I read it to your honour?"

Without tarrying a reply, he began to rummage a parcel of papers—swearing between whiles, and grumbling to himself—till at last, he exclaimed:

"I believe *ould* nick has set his foot upon it!"

"What! have you lost it?" demanded his master.

"No; but I can't find it, my lord.—Hey? Och! Saint Patrick be praised! here it is."

He gave two or three hems, by way of clearing his throat; and in a tone as monotonous as the sound of a penny drum, read the following.

"*Honourable* Father and Mother:

"This comes to let you know, you will receive it—unless it miscarries on the way—as a countryman of our's (who was born here) has promised to deliver it himself by the hands of his father. I am alive and in sound health at this present writing; and so is my master—who, poor gentleman! is half dead, with a hole that has been drilled through his body by one of these whisker-faced Dons. There he is at death's door, with nothing but Murdoch's prayers, and Saint Patrick to keep him: and I am mighty fearful, the gentleman's interest is not so good here as it is in Ireland.

"But, in order to make myself perfectly *incomprehensible*, it will be the shortest way to give you a full and concise abridgement of the whole affair; or, as you may more properly call it, a *cullender* of our expedition.

"We were taking a *tower* on two mules, (a kind of *amphibious crature*, with ears like a *donky*) when we were overtaken by a parcel of ill-looking fellows, who met us on the road, and run about these mountains, like tame rabbits in a warren. So, without saying a word, they bid us deliver our money, and fixed their blunderbusses in our faces; which happened to miss us both—or it might have hit us. For my own part I would have given 'em all mine in a crack—for the devil a brass farthing I had about me in all the world; so that, if they had had it for nothing, they would not have made much by their bargain: but my master (good luck to him!) swore they should not have the price of a rope from him, and fired a good-looking pistol at 'em—so did myself—his servant. Pop! pop! pop! went the shot, like rounds of whiskey at a wake, till my poor lord came tumbling to the ground, like a load of shot *murphies*. Now, thinks I to myself, good bye to us both!—But in this strange *dillyme*, some gentlemen came up; and the thieves (like no true men, as they were) ran away: we were then taken to the castle of an ould Count, hard by; and here we have been ever since, voluntarily, and against my master's free will.

"Now was not this mighty uncivil, honies, to attack two strange passengers, in the dark, by moonlight, and put them in bodily fear, on the highway?—Och! the house-breakers! I should not wonder if they came to an untimely end!—But they think so little of suicide here, that they murder a fellow-crature, with as much composure as you'd lap up a mess of buttermilk.—Where can their religion be, and be damned to 'em!—Then they have a mighty ugly way of *boddering* a parcel of dumb *baists* to death, at what they call their faists; and *kill bulls* here faster than we *make* 'em in Ireland.

"Well, after this escape, which was as good as a reprieve to a man at the gallows, away is his lordship going to fight with the Moors of Granada. The war is something about religion; but it is an odd thing to me, that cutting throats should be thought a ready way of going to heaven!

"I shall write again as soon as we are in camp; which will not be long I suppose—for my lord is never at peace but when he is going to war; and I look upon it he will take to his heels, the instant the surgeon has set him on his legs. Where the camp is I can't exactly tell; *becase* I don't know —being a stranger to the navigation of this country; which is not very wonderful, considering I never was in it before.

"Depend on hearing from me as often as possible, considering I am on the other side of the water: but if I should be *kilt* by these barbarous blackamoors, that we are going to fisty-cuffs with, I hope you'll excuse my future silence. Dear honies! do send me your blessing in your next (as you have not written to me yet) and pray for the salvation of

your dutiful,

and *tender*-loving son

MURDOCH MC. CLUDDEROUGH.

"*P. S.* You will receive in a very short time, a pistole (which is worth a little more than a mark) and it will come free of all expense, except the carriage—and that won't cost you more than two or three and twenty thirteeners.—My respects to Colley the cow, and the *ould* black *mud-lark*."

"There, my lord," cried Murdoch, with an air of triumph, "is not that the dandy?—If ever there was a piece of poetry, I know nothing of arithmetic, at all, at all."

"I confess," replied his lordship, "it is beyond my calculations to ascertain your meaning; but you know it yourself and that is sufficient."

"Och! quite sufficient, Sir. But I have got the *subscription* to add at the top of the back, and then it is done."

He directed it thus:

"*For Mr. and Mrs. Mc. Cludderough, Fruiterers and Timber*

Merchants, at the sign of the Nutshell and Tooth-ache, in the town of Kildare, in the Province of Ireland."

"Very well," said Lord Liffey—having read it: "but it is the first time I knew your parents were timber-merchants and fruiterers."

"Och! your honour, don't you know that the dear honies deal in birch-brooms and potatoes?—Well, there it is—finished to the very end; and my poor dad and mam will get it in a crack—for a good-natured Spaniard (who says he is of Irish *distraction*) that is to take it, is only going on a bit of a voyage to the other—hubbubboo! I mean, to the *new* world; and he has promised me that immediately on his return, he will deliver it; or, at any rate send it to Mr. and Mrs. Mc. Cludderough—so that, you know, there can be no delay, your honour."

"By Saint Patrick! you grow more and more incorrigible!" said his lordship.—"Send a letter to Ireland by a man who is going on a voyage of discoveries? Dolt! tarry till I send my own letters, and your curious epistle shall accompany them."

"Ah! good luck to your honour! don't cast no disparagements on my *larning*!" cried Murdoch.—"It is well known that all my family, male and female, have been men of letters, and made some noise in the world: for my great-grandfather was crier of Kilkenny, and my uncle was parish-clerk of Wexford—and, moreover, I had a cousin who was a trumpeter in a regiment of horse. As for my way of sending my letter, I am not the first man that of two ways, has taken the wrong: and let 'em say what they will of Irishmen's mistakes, I am sure, it is something in the air; and I am very positive, if any other countryman was to be born there, he would be just as good at blundering as the rankest Murphy that ever tippled whiskey."

CHAP. IX.

O! conspiracy!
Sham'st thou to shew thy dangerous face by night,
When evils are most free?

JULIUS CÆSAR.[1]

But see, his face is black, and full of blood!
His eye-balls further out than when he liv'd:
Staring full ghastly, like a strangled man!
His hair up-rear'd, his nostrils strain'd with struggling!
His hands abroad display'd, as one that graspt
And tugg'd for life, and was by strength subdu'd
Look on the sheets; his hair you see is sticking,
His well-proportion'd beard made rough and rugged,
Like to the summer's corn, by tempest lodg'd.
It cannot be, but he was murder'd here:
The least of all these signs were probable.

2nd PART OF KING HENRY VIIth[2]

IT was at the close of a drizzling, cheerless day, as Lewis was passing through the picture-gallery, that he heard the soft tread of footsteps, ascending a private staircase, with much caution. He was at a loss to conceive the motive for such circumspection: and, hiding himself in a place, where he thought he was secure from observation, beheld Rodorigo and another man gain the head of the stairs, and proceed to the apartment of the former—the door of which they closed and bolted. If Lewis was in the first instance surprised to see his young lord approach with such secrecy,

---

1 Shakespeare, *Julius Caesar* (1599), 2.1.78-80.
2 Shakespeare, *Henry VI Part Two* (1591), 3.2.168-174.

and with a stranger, how was that surprise augmented, when in that stranger he remembered the features of an old acknowledged ruffian, named Volponé! This man inhabited a cottage not far from the castle; he was said to be a villain capable of the most atrocious crimes, and whose subsistence was chiefly owing to depredation.

"Here must be some wrong going forward," said Lewis to himself: "but by Saint Iago! I shall take the liberty to lend an ear to your discourse!"

He advanced on tiptoe, and applying his ear to the key-hole, overheard the following dialogue.

"Yes, Volponé," said the Count's son, "before I pour my purpose in your ear, you must bind yourself by an oath, strong as the mind of man can furnish. Therefore, bethink thee."

"To the point, Signor," replied Volponé: "I never was fond of a long preface; and since you don't think proper to trust me without an oath, propose one, and then to business."

"Nay, understand me: the business I am about to put on you, demands the resolution of a man," said the son of Antonio.

"And you will not find me a milksop, that will shrink from it, be it what it may," returned the other; "so to the point."

"Wish," said Rodorigo, "that your limbs may lose their function, and wither into nothing, the instant you betray me!"

"I do wish it, my lord!" quoth Volponé—"I swear I never will!"

"Enough.—Know then," rejoined Rodorigo, in a low voice, "know then——"

At that instant, old Lewis's heels (from the glibness of the polished oaken boards and the position in which he stood) flew from under him; and he came to the ground with no small noise. He gathered his limbs up with more agility than he had lately moved, and crawled on his hands and knees to a niche, wherein was a statue of Pluto, behind which he deposited himself; his teeth chattering with terror, and cursing his own curiosity.

Hardly had he concealed himself, when Rodorigo issued from his room, his sword drawn, and followed by Volponé; and casting a glance around, cried:

"Whence was that noise?"

"I know not, my lord: all is silent, and I am apt to think we were deceived by fancy," said the other.

"Impossible! my ears could not be grossly duped; more like some prying fool, intent upon the secrets of others," rejoined Rodorigo. "But, by the Virgin! if I discover him, I'll mar his curiosity!"

He examined great part of the gallery, and passed by the niche wherein old Lewis lay, ague-stricken (and which was the only one he did not look into) when expressing his indignation that they had escaped his vengeance, he returned to his chamber. Then Lewis, shaking like an aspen-leaf, crawled from his ambush; and falling on his knees before the statue, poured out his gratitude to this effect:

"Oh! Pluto! good king of hell! receive my thanks!— Thou hast been my saviour; and never shall I see thy devil-ship's face, but with reverence! and, moreover, if I run my nose into the secrets of others again, may it be served as puppies' tails are, and twisted from my phiz!"

Then, like a dog that had escaped from the rabble, he glided down the great stair-case, without turning his head, lest his eyes should encounter Rodorigo—than whom he would rather have encountered Satan himself. Having gained the buttery, he sought to prop up his spirits with a flask of Malaga: but though his fears had for the time banished them, his suspicions recurred with accumulated force, and he prognosticated some disaster to be at hand; in which idea he was not far from right.

It happened, that the same night, Hilario and Carlos had a violent dispute; in the course of which, the former unhandsomely told him of his dependent state, and of the favours he had received from the Count.—Carlos fired at this unmanly insult, and was about to retort, but the presence of the ladies checked him; and he replied, he was not to be insulted with impunity, but, that Don Hilario should, *ere long, severely atone his insolence.*—Then, in opposition to the united entreaties of the company, he retired.

On the subsequent morning, when the family met at breakfast, Carlos and Hilario not being present, Lewis was dispatched to their chambers to summon them.

"I hope," said the Count, "we shall be able to reconcile those hot-brained boys: 'tis a pity they should have fallen out, for they are both fine spirited youths."

"They are so," replied Lord Liffey; "but Don Hilario was the aggressor, and I doubt not will apologize for his conduct: for surely 'tis as meritorious to make a concession for an inadvertency, as it is to resent a real insult. I am from a country where these affairs are accommodated, but by the death of one of the parties: yet I must own, I never could discover, how running a man through the body, should be a satisfaction for having previously insulted him."

He was interrupted by Lewis, who rushed into the room, and threw himself into a chair; his eyes rolling—his hair standing on end—and marks of blood upon his face.

"What is the matter?" demanded the Count.

"He's gone! he's gone! he's gone!" repeated Lewis, empathetically.

"Who is gone, and what do you mean?" inquired Antonio.

"Oh! miserable old man that I am!" exclaimed the steward, not attending to the interrogatory: "that I should live to see these doings! I rather would have died forty years ago!"

"Explain this mystery, I command you!" interrupted the Count.

"I beg your lordship's pardon;—I'll tell you—I'll tell you all—if I can," quoth Lewis. "I went, according to your order, to call Don Carlos; but he was not in his room, nor had he lain in his bed.—Well (mercy on me; I can hardly tell it!) I thought that strange; but what followed—Oh! I shudder while I think of it! I then went to Don Hilario's chamber—knocked, but received no answer—I opened the door, and called upon his name; but, all being silent, I unclosed the curtains—and there—I beg your pardon my lord! I cannot proceed—I—"

They stared at each other, every one ignorant whither this could tend to: at length Lord Liffey broke the silence.

" 'Tis in vain," said he, "to seek intelligence from this old man; his fears have overcome him. Let us go to the apartment of Don Hilario, and try to unravel this mystery."

This being assented to, they proceeded to the chamber; and there a spectacle saluted their eyes, that filled them with horror inexpressible—for they beheld the corpse of unhappy Hilario stretched on the bed, and bathed in his own blood!

"Who should have committed this accursed deed?" cried the general.

"Accursed, indeed!" repeated Liffey. "Ill-fated Hilario! may I be allowed to avenge you!—You see his throat is cut from ear to ear! and his right hand nearly deprived of the fingers! in grasping the instrument of death no doubt, while struggling for existence!—His hair (horrible!) is clotted to the sheets! Ha! what is here! By heaven! the very scarf Don Carlos wore but yesterday!—Merciful God! can he, to satiate his malice, have stooped to the act of an assassin?"

They examined the scarf, and each in wonder owned it was the same they had seen Carlos wear: and now the son of Count Antonio addressed them—declaring, that before the discovery of this dumb evidence, he had in his own mind convicted its owner of the murder. This suggestion was opposed by Don Hannibal; who (as was usual with him) dropt some expressions not much in his nephew's favour.

To this, Rodorigo closely answered:

"I am not ignorant, that any observation of mine is sure to meet with my uncle's decided opposition; 'though, how I have been so unfortunate as to incur his continual displeasure, I am yet to learn. Be that as it may—I shall not, even at the hazard of his disapprobation, withhold my sentiments—which force me to repeat Don Carlos the author of this bloody tragedy. I appeal to all present, whether my accusation be founded upon reason?—Reflect on the last night's quarrel—reflect how ineffectual were all endeavours to restrain the transports of Carlos, as with bitter and vindictive threats, he burst from the room—and above all, think of his sudden absence! These facts considered, answer me, and seriously, who can one moment hesitate to pronounce him guilty?"

"I can! I do!" replied Hannibal. "I never will prejudge any man; or hold him guilty, till his country's laws have found him so."

"Enough! enough! it is too plain!" cried the Count, who with folded arms, had been gazing on the melancholy spectacle in speechless horror. "The scarf (torn and bloody as it is) must have been dragged from the shoulder of the assassin by the deceased, while in the agonies of death. It shocks my nature to think the earth should teem with such a monster!"

Observing the Count to be much affected, they begged him to retire, and were about to force him from this scene of horror; when Agnes, half-breathless, rushed into the room, and uttering a piercing scream, fell insensible upon the mangled body!

There we shall leave her, and accompany the cavaliers (with the exception of Don Hannibal) to the hall; who after a short consultation, dispatched horsemen several ways in pursuit of the murderer. That done, Rodorigo thus harangued them.

"I am," said he, "compelled to make a proposal that wrings my heart, as it will separate me from my father, at a time when he stands in most need of my attention. But justice urges me, and I obey. The greatest sceptic I believe, can entertain no doubt as to Don Carlos' guilt. How callous then, and lost to every sentiment of gratitude and humanity must be the heart of that wretch, who could contaminate the roof of his benefactor with the blood of his guest! Should not such a villain be hunted through the world? Be held up to the execration of mankind—and brought to the punishment of those laws he has so grossly violated?—Now to my purpose: I am well persuaded the murderer will instantly join the army, as a situation most secure from apprehension. The royal standard is planted without the walls of Seville: hither Lord Liffey, as he informed us yesterday, sets out to-morrow; and I will with him—in hopes of finding the homicide, and (under heaven's favour) bringing him to justice."

To this proposal the Count, though unwillingly, gave his acquiescence; and Liffey and Rodorigo having fixed their departure for the subsequent morning, the former retired to his apartment; whither he was attended by his servant, and joined by Buzzardo.

"I come to ask a favour," said he. " 'Tis brief; for I hate long stories: I am determined to leave this abominable place; and having a relation at Seville, I shall be happy to join your party."

"The favour will be conferred on us. But shall you be able to undergo the *fatigue* of such a journey?" demanded his lordship, with a smile.

"I'd undergo a voyage to the Antipodes, rather than stay in this *slaughter-house*," returned Buzzardo, with some little energy. "Who knows (but the Virgin forbid) it may be my turn to have my throat cut next!"

"Make yourself easy on that score, Signor; for you'll never live to see that day," cried Murdoch.

"I hope not," said Buzzardo: "but here I can't remain; for the fright would kill me in a week."

"Then you are right to be missing," rejoined Murdoch: "for a man may as well be killed, as frightened to death, at any time. And you may save your bacon by carrying it away with you: for perhaps it's the same here as it is in little Ireland."

"How's that?" enquired the don.

"By J—! they never hang a man there 'till they've *catched* him!—By my soul! 'though this is such bloody work, that I would not wonder if we all got our *quiatus* one night, and did not find out we were put to sleep in earnest, 'till we awoke next morning.

"Am I to be eternally troubled with your ridiculous observation and conjectures?" said his master.

"No, Sir; and if they go on at this rate, we shall not trouble one another long. As for my ridiculous observations, my lord, there's more truth in them than you think for. Murdoch's horse (my namesake, and King of Ulster, by the by) in a bit of a *skrimidch* with the enemy, met with the trifling accident of losing his head; after which, the spirited *baist* trotted five miles full gallop, till coming to a bit of a brook, and finding the roof of his mouth parched, he stooped to drink, and found by his shadow that he had lost his head!"

"I should imagine the loss the poor beast sustained had been entailed on all who bore his owner's name: at least if I may judge of you as a sample—for you've no more head than—"

"A smooth *thirteener*," interrupted Murdoch—"I ask your honour's pardon, but I saw you was struck fast in the mud for want of a *caparison*."

"Leave the room!" cried Liffey, in an authoritative tone.

Murdoch obeyed, bowing and retired; and as he closed the door, said to himself—

"My lord certainly has the advantage over me in point of authority; but, in the way of facts and arguments, I flatter myself, there are very few who can hold a candle to Mr. Mc. Cludderough."

Next morning, our travellers were ready for their journey; and after an almost silent meal, repaired to the courtyard, where their horses waited for them. The Marchioness of Valencia bade Rodorigo adieu, and solicited his early return, with a sorrowful air; which did not escape the observation of Liffey, who afterwards rallied him on it severely. The Count clasping his son in his arms, and sobbing his farewell, was so overcome by his feelings, that he could hardly support himself; and when the latter vaulted into his saddle, the old man laid his hand upon Lewis's shoulder and wept aloud. The noise of the horses' hoofs in leaving the courtyard aroused him: leaning on the steward's arm, he past the gate, and followed his son (now, perhaps his only son!) with his eyes, till an intervening rock robbed him of the sight—then re-entered the castle gloomy and disconsolate.

CHAP. X.

> But now, t'observe Romantick Method,
> Let bloody steel awhile be sheathed.—
>
> HUDIBRAS.[1]

NOTHING material occurred to our travellers, during the first two days of their journey; in which, Don Buzzardo complained bitterly of the length of the way, and Murdoch frequently took the liberty to remind his lord, how different the geography of Spain was to that of their own country—the dear land of potatoes.—

On the second night they halted at a solitary inn; at the door of which they knocked till their patience was almost exhausted. At length it was opened by the landlord; who, on understanding they wanted refreshment, and meant to stop all night, began to call about him—"Here, Michael! Lissardo! &c."—Though it was ascertained, his whole family consisted of himself, a daughter, and one serving man. Receiving no answer, he began to be angry; 'till the hostler (for as such he was to act on the present occasion) made his appearance, and took charge of the horses. The landlord now begged his guests to follow him, and moved on in a rather serpentine direction, to what he called a parlour—but, which seemed to have served as an eating-room for half the pigs in the province.

All eyes were fixed on him. He was about five feet high; of the rotundity of one of his own butts—and a visage of that crimson glow, that any spectator might have aptly said—

1 Samuel Butler (1613-1680), *Hudibras Part Two* (1664), 1-2.

I never look upon thy face, but it puts me in mind of hell's fires.[1]

He was stupidly intoxicated—and leaning his back against the wall, he began to hiccup his apologies, for the time he had detained them at the door.

"I am extre—re (hic!) emely sorry, Signor Cavalieros, I should have kept you so long.—But what can I do?—I have a swarm of idle dogs about the house, who take their siesta with as much consequence as the first hidalgo in the country; and not con—con (hic!) tented with that—snore half the rest of the day besides. A plague! (hic!) a plague upon 'em! I'm never to be at peace! I did think when I buried my wife (I hope she enjoys the rest she denied me!) that there was pro—ro—(hic!) robality of my enjoying a little quiet. But no; I'm as much plagued now as I was then: for to do the dear woman justice, she not only kept her own tongue, but every creature in the house in motion."

"Yaw!" cried Buzzardo, stretching himself—"heaven be praised! here we are at last!"

"Yes, your honours—here you are—(hic!) as safe as bottles in saw-dust—and now, if you'll take a little sober advice, you'll have a delicate bit of supper, a glass of wine that can't be equalled in the king's cellar, and then to bed."

"As to sober advice, I shall have no objection to it," said Liffey—"providing you have any body at hand to give it."

"Your honour's a wag!" returned the host: "but as it is a cheap bill of fare (for it costs nothing) I'll give you a little of that commo—mo—hic!—modity."

"*You* give sober advice?" exclaimed Murdoch. "By my soul! it would be like Connor of Connaught, that gave his money away after he had none left for himself!—Arrah! don't be after making a *Judy* of yourself—you're drunk, man."

1 Shakespeare, *Henry IV Part One* (1597), 3.3.26-27.

"Drunk?" repeated the landlord, with a vacant stare.

"As a fiddler's dog, or a horse with the staggers."

"Come I like that! I'm a perfect pattern of sobri—ri—ri—hic!—riety; and I'll defy the oldest acquaintance I have in the world, to say he ever saw me otherwise than I am at this moment," said mine host with a stagger.

"Upon my conscience! I believe you!" said Liffey. "And should any one contradict the assertion, that garnet-studded nose and ruby cheek of thine, will give them the lie."

"Yes—I'll give 'em the lie," muttered the inn-keeper. "But to return to the supper—what would you like, hidal-gos?—Something delicate?"

"As we are come unexpectedly upon you, we must be content with what we can get," said Liffey. "What *can* you give us?"

"I'll tell you, Signor, and that without any circumlo—lo—hic!—cution. Meteor is not like many innkeepers, that praise what they had such a day, and such a day; but keep you in the dark about what they have got now. No—I like to be expli—li—hic!—licit—and to throw a light upon the business at once."

"Which you cannot fail to do, if the reflection of your own face falls upon it," observed Liffey; "for thou art my *Aurora Borealis*. But to the point: what have you to eat?"

"There's the remains of a barbecued pig, and an olla-podrida, richly seasoned with garlic, if you could fancy it."

"Delicate eating, by the mass!" cried Liffey.

"Why, Signor, it's not *over* strong. At least, I dare say, you'll not find it so, for you are a soldier: and they tell me, you soldiers have the stoutest stomachs of any under the sun."

"And I trust they will never have cause to say otherwise," replied his lordship. "We have had some strong dishes prepared for us by our foes; but they have never turned our stomachs, nor will we turn our backs upon 'em."

"That's just what I say to my friend, here," said Meteor, taking out his flask, and drinking. "You have never turned my stomach, and I'll be damned if ever I turn my back upon you!"

So saying, he reeled out of the room, but returned with his daughter, bringing in the barbecue and olla-podrida, which was too *delicately* relished for the palates of his guests: the wine too was such, that his assertion, of its not having its *equal*, was indubitable still, his own panegyrics on the several commodities were without effect—his company ate sparingly: but for this he consoled himself (as most of his vocation do) with the recollection, that—*they would pay the same.*

Dissatisfied with their treatment, the party retired, and the house had been in perfect silence about an hour, mine host and Murdoch snoring over their wine, in the kitchen, when Liffey left his bed, and stole towards that of his landlord's daughter. Jacintha was a strapping rosy wench, with hair like a raven, teeth like ivory, and eyes like——no matter what. No wonder then, that our young Hibernian, full of health and vigour, should cast an eye of desire upon her; and that the accusation of chastity never having been brought against the lady, she should listen to his tale of love, and even make an assignation with him, in her own room—

When all were wrapt in sleep!

Liffey lay, thinking every minute an age 'till all was quiet; when, as we have said, he arose, and found his way to the chamber of Jacintha. She was in bed: into which he also hastened, and had just caught her in his arms, when three gentle taps at the door, caused his partner to exclaim:

"Jesu Maria! there's my father I suppose!"

Liffey objected at first to quit his station; but she professed and exhibited such consternation, that he consented to conceal himself beneath the bed, till the intruder should have retired.

The door was opened, and it being entirely dark, he lent all ears to ascertain the conversation; when they were assailed by the voice of Don Buzzardo—who was there on a similar errand to himself. Irritated at his disappointment, he vowed revenge—and, as the luckless wight raised one foot to the bed, he seized the other, and squeezed it with such *Herculean* force, that poor Buzzardo roared aloud, with pain and terror. Liffey then extricated himself from his place of concealment and absconded; but the cries of the Spaniard awakened Meteor and his companion, and they hurried upstairs to learn the cause of the alarm. Jacintha, hearing footsteps and fearing her incontinence would be discovered, determined by a stroke of policy to prevent it; and grasping Buzzardo hard, exclaimed vociferously:

"Help! murder! ravishment!"

Mine host rushed into the room, followed by Murdoch—and seeing his daughter struggling with a man, seized a certain *chamber utensil*, and discharged the contents on the head of the ill-starred Buzzardo—who stood trembling with terror, and drenched with wet, no bad emblem of an ill-carved river god.

"Oh! my good father!" cried the artful girl—"how opportunely you are come to save your daughter's virtue!—This brute, for I can't call him any thing else, broke open my door; and God knows what might have been the consequence, if you had not come to my relief!"

"A brute indeed! I suppose he is drunk—for no *sober* man would attempt such an atro—ro—ro—(hic!)—rocious thing," muttered the half-muzzy father. "I've often said, liquor is the ruin of thousands. But mind me, *Signor Amo-*

roso! return to your bed, and don't attempt the like again; or I shall toss you out of the window, with less ceremony than I would an empty flask."

Buzzardo did not think it politic to tarry a repetition of this command, but retired—cursing his own folly in attempting so troublesome a job as that of a chamber-maid's chastity. The next day the party resumed their journey; the Don having no inclination to renew his intended encounter with the buxom Jacintha—with whom Liffey nevertheless had contrived to pass the remainder of the night.

CHAP. XI.

O! Lady, he's dead and gone!
Lady he's dead and gone!
And at his head a green grass turf,
And at his heels a stone!

THE FRIAR OF ORDERS GREY.[1]

AGNES, cold and inanimate as the mangled body of her brother, on which she had fallen, was conveyed to her own chamber; where Aurora attended her with the anxiety of a fond sister. Her own happiness had received a mortal blow in the sanguinary villainy of her lover, and she sought to soothe her feelings by administering the balm of comfort to her friend.

Many hours did the sister of Hilario remain lifeless —when she raised herself in bed, and glaring round the room with a vacant eye, cried:

"Will no one punish yon vile miscreant?—See where he wings his way—his plumage dropping blood!—I saw the

---

1 Thomas Percy (1729-1811), from *Reliques of Ancient English Poetry* (1765), 17-20.

deed committed!—A turtle and his mate died long since, and left two of their young brood behind them—one of which was male, and to his care did they consign the other. He loved her dearly (or I have lost the tale) and was beloved by her. Their nest was humble; but contentment strewed her down upon it, and they were blest in each other.—Ah! why did they ever quit it!—Safety and peace at home—abroad, danger and turmoil!—While absent from their nest, a vulture saw and envied them their bliss —pounced on the male, and struck his crooked talons to his heart—the life-stream followed, and he died. But mark! the unhappy—she (deprived of her protector) pines alone, making the groves re-echo to her moans, and no one goes to comfort her.——Ah! I will go in search of my brother; he shall destroy the monster.——Soft! soft! soft! did not you tell me he was gone on a long journey?——But he will come back; for I know he loves his Agnes too well to leave her long, and till he comes, we'll sit and tell each *other* tales of misery!"

She continued in this state of insanity, during the whole of that day, and the next: on the second evening she regarded Aurora and the Marchioness with a delirious look, and said:

"You told me you would bring my brother—but no matter; I am going where he is, and shall see him very soon. This is my bridal night: let me be arrayed in white— let the neighbouring maidens strew the way with flowers —and let the convent-bell announce my coming thither. My nuptial bed shall be a coffin, a cold vault my chamber, and the grim tyrant, who wields the scythe of life, my bridegroom: for my thoughts are gloomy, and I pant for the embrace of death!—Attend the banquet ladies; and from mouldering skulls—quaff life-blood to our sheets!— The night is very stormy! how the wind whistles! and the

lightning slashes!—Ha! what form is that?—It is my dear
Hilario! see how his wounds gape!—He smiles—and
beckons me to follow him!—Blest shade! lead on! e'en to
eternity, I am your's!"

She endeavoured to rise, but her exertions had
exhausted her, and she sunk articulating in a low voice,
something about her brother—and at last dropped into a
slumber—interrupted by convulsive spasms, and heart-
fetched sighs.

The Marchioness now took leave of Aurora, for the
night—when the latter, exhausted with long watching, fell
into a sound sleep, from which, the castle-clock striking
twelve, awoke her. The lights burnt dimly in the sockets,
and the bed was situated in a recess, where the faint gleam
hardly penetrated. She took a taper, and gently drew aside
the curtains, when she shrunk back with horror, screamed,
and dropt upon the floor.

Lewis happened to be passing through the gallery at
the time, and without the ceremony of knocking, went
in, seeing his young lady on the ground, he rang the bell
violently—which was answered by two servants, one of
whom he dispatched to desire his lord's immediate presence.

The good old man then knelt by the side of Aurora,
and chafed her temples with water, till she revived—and
with his assistance arose.—She looked round the room
with anxiety—and seeing the window open, exclaimed in
extreme terror:—

"Oh! my God! is it even so!" Then she snatched the taper
from Lewis, darted out of the room, and rushed like lightning past her uncle, whom she met on the stairs.—The
Count called to her to stop, but in vain—she pursued her
way with the same velocity, nor paused until she gained
the inner court, where bruised and mangled lay the bleed-

ing corse of the late beauteous Agnes.

The Count found her with the head of the deceased on her knee, and the clay-cold hand pressed to her own lips.

"Father of mercy!" cried he, "more blood!—Where will they end?"

He averted his head, and hid it on the shoulder of his faithful steward, who was himself overpowered with grief and dismay—while the servants crowded forward to gaze on the scene, and the beams of the torches glared full upon the livid features of the departed maid.

"Oh! Agnes!" said Aurora, "friend of my youth! and beloved of my heart! is thy life nipped in the very bud?— Are all those heavenly graces, which were united in thee, doomed to an end like this?"

"Cease!" cried the Count, "dear child of my affection! cease this storm of grief!—Thou know'st not how it wounds me!"

"Ah! my dear uncle! can I behold this lovely girl, stript of early life, and not lament the loss?—Behold those eyes which used to beam with heavenly emanation, now set in death!—Those lips, whereon a smile was wont to play, and enliven all around her—are now sealed for ever!—Alas! what havock has that insatiate tyrant made in this sweet paragon of nature!"

"This sorrow is amiable," said the Count—"but it will not revive the dead. Have mercy, then, upon the living; and do not my adored Aurora! add to the weight of thy uncle's grief, which already bids fair to bend him to the grave!"

"Forgive me my adored parent! (so I may surely call you) I will calm my transports," returned Aurora. "I will not give way to the foolishness of woe, but I will strive to merit thy unbounded kindness."

She threw herself on his neck, and they mingled tears as they returned into the castle.

The bodies of the ill-fated brother and sister were removed to the castle of Hara, and afterwards interred in the monastery of Saint James—where their melancholy tale is still rehearsed to the inquiring traveller.

END OF VOL. I.

THE

MYSTIC SEPULCHRE;

OR,

SUCH THINGS HAVE BEEN.

A Spanish Romance.

IN TWO VOLUMES.

By JOHN PALMER,

Author of the " Haunted Cavern"—" Mystery of the Black Tower"—" World as it goes," &c.

" 'TWAS BUT MY FANCY !"—

King Richard the Third.

VOL. II.

London.

Printed by J. Nichols, Earl's-court, Leicester Square.

FOR W. EARLE,

ALBEMARLE-STREET, PICCADILLY.

. . . .

1807.

CHAP. I.

Women! help heaven! men their creation mar
In profiting by them: nay, call us ten times frail,
For we are soft as our complexions are,
And credulous to false prints.

MEASURE FOR MEASURE.[1]

O! who does know the bent of woman's fantasies?

SPENSER.[2]

Now to return to our travellers.

At the distance of a league from Seville, they passed through a village where Lord Liffey seemed to regard a good-looking house, on the right side of the road, with very earnest attention. The upper windows were latticed—while those of the lower story were concealed by a lofty wall.

"You see that house?" observed his lordship. "That place was the scene of two or three as whimsical incidents to me, as are met with in the common occurrences of life. I am (like most of my countrymen) a sad bungler at a story —but if you will not think your time ill-bestowed, I will repeat the circumstances to which I allude."

His companions giving their assent, he began.

"Some three years ago," said he—"I attended vespers at one of the churches in Seville—where I saw a young lady of such uncommon beauty (as I ascertained from a

---

1 Shakespeare, *Measure for Measure* (1623), 2.4.127-130.
2 Edmund Spenser (1552/1553-1599), *The Faerie Queene* (1590), Book I, Canto IV, 216.

transient view, by the accidental removal of her veil) that I went home deeply captivated.

"The following day I waited on my banker for a supply of money. He was an avaricious old wretch, married to a young wife, from whom he was in eternal dread of cuckoldom and therefore he secreted her from the knowledge of all his acquaintance.

"Observing me not to be in my accustomed spirits, he inquired the reason, and whether some of the beauties of Seville had not *drawn upon my heart at sight?*

"I told him he was right: that I had seen a beautiful woman at church on the preceding evening, and would give the world for another interview—of which, however I despaired—as the crowd had separated us, and I had no clue to guide me to her.

'Pooh! Pooh!' cried the old man—'you a soldier and despair? follow my counsel—and if it don't turn to account, never take a draft of advice, to which Cornuto's name is affixed, again. Go to the same church this evening, (I warrant your fair incognita will be there) station yourself near her, and take care the crowd don't again intervene. Follow her home—and should you not have an opportunity to breathe any soft nonsense into her ear in the way, beset her door, as an alquazil would a place of sanctuary, that contained a criminal. Your perseverance will catch her attention—she will appear at a window or elsewhere, and you will be able to let her know by signs the state of your heart. Don't let the idea of being too extravagant in your gestures assail you, but give her to understand you cannot live without her. Women love to affect compassion: the thought of averting your death will be a healing plaister to her conscience—or in other words, a good excuse for following her own inclination. I know the sex—and know the only method of keeping them content is by putting it out of their power to be otherwise. Mark me! *I say out of their power!*—Well, what you think of my advice?'

"I liked it so well, that I resolved to put it into execution —and prayed heaven it might succeed.

"I accordingly attended vespers—and had the satisfaction to behold the same lovely stranger. I followed her out of church—but the presence of an elderly female (who had also before accompanied her) prevented my profiting further by the sight of her, than by tracing her home— which I did to the house we have just passed.

"I beset the place many days, for many hours—often having the pleasure to see her at the upper windows, and flattering myself she did not regard my gesticulations with disdain.—One day I saw the old woman who had attended her at church, come out of the garden gate. This, said I, is my lucky minute—or perhaps never. I went to her, and was upon the point of accosting her—when the harridan drew herself up, pulled her veil over her face, and demanded my business. To this I replied, my business was of a nature that required a thousand apologies, which love must make for me, and that the boldness (if so she should deem it) of the favour I was about to ask, must be imputed to the influence of that omnipotent Deity.

'*Favour?*' repeated she, empathetically. 'What do you mean by that? do you take Donna Ursula, Salina de Mustachio for a courtesan?—I understand your wicked thoughts —but what do you see about me that should tempt you to ask a favour of me?'

"Nothing, *on your own account*—thought I: for the glimpse I got of her at church, convinced me she was as ugly as the devil—and I soon discovered she was as vain as ugly, and as ignorant as vain. I informed her of her error, in imagining I had any design on her person, and presented her with a diamond ring, saying, all I requested was, that she would indulge me with five minutes conversation with the *other* young lady, resident in the house with herself.

"She fixed her eyes upon the ring, and told me, I had such a handsome way of making a present, as well as asking a *favour* (and she begged me to believe, that had it been such as she had conjectured, it would not be the *first* time of her having experienced the like application) that she could not refuse me. 'You are a foreigner I perceive,' concluded she, 'and from your gallant manner I should suppose you a Frenchman.'

"*Och!* blood and turf!" cried Murdoch, who was in the rear of the company, and heard his master's story, "did the *ould* devil take you for a Frenchman?—You that have got a brogue the king might be mighty proud of!"

"Be quiet Murdoch, and don't give your tongue so much licence!" said Lord Liffey—and he proceeded.

"I told her I *was* a Frenchman,"—Murdoch groaned —"that I came from a county called Kilkenny, and was descendant of the great Monsieur Tamerlane, the Tartar —whose progeny had since settled in France—and finished with a rhapsody in the *Erse* language. To this she made answer, that she had forgot most of her French, and therefore requested I would not *again* address her in that language: said, she knew a Frenchman of the same county as myself, and had often heard my family named as a very great one. She bade me be at the garden-gate at ten o'clock that night, and she would admit me. I returned her my thanks, and left her—I, elated to the spheres!

"You may be sure I was punctual to my assignation— and was met at the garden-gate by Ursula, and conducted to a small elegant apartment.

'Ah! monsieur,' said the old woman, 'I am glad to find you so exact. You are the image of my poor dead husband. To be sure you have the advantage—but bating that he squinted, had a small rise between his shoulders, and that one of his legs were made *cheese-cutter* fashion, you are the *moral* of him. Ah! I wish he was alive!—Though I believe the dear man is as well where he is, for all that.—By the Virgin! I could love you for his sake!'

"She took hold of my hand, languished with a pair of rheumy eyes, and gave me to understand she was not so hard-hearted as she wished at first to appear to me. I, however, was too impatient to see the object of my wishes, to be entertained with her absurdities, and interrupted her abruptly, with—My good woman! this is all very fine—but we delay time by it. Where is the lady with whom you promised me an interview?

'Good woman?' repeated she, with a disdainful toss of the head. 'I'd have you to know, *Monsieur*, this is the first time I ever was called by that name. But your sex are all alike—ungrateful!—I have made a point never to refuse *any thing* that the filthy men have asked of me, and they have all repaid my kindness in the same way!'

"She flounced out of the room, muttering, that *the world was come to a fine pass*, when girls, hardly out of their leading strings were preferred to women who had *nearly* attained their maturity.

"She made ample compensation for this sally, by returning with my charming angel: to whom she presented me, saying:

'This, Signora Stella, is *Monsieur Tamarind*, the French Tartar, that I told you of.'

"I smiled at her ignorance, but interrupted her eloquence and said every thing my passion could suggest, to convince Stella of my attachment. She heard me with attention, and vouchsafed to say my professions were not unpleasing to her. I had passed one of the pleasantest hours of my life, and began to hug myself on my good fortune, when a loud ringing at the gate made Stella start from her seat, and exclaim:

'Jesu! there's my husband!'

'Then I'm a dead woman if the Tartar is found here!' exclaimed Ursula. 'Hide yourself for the love of the Virgin!'

"No, said I—if I do hide myself, it shall be for the love of the *wife*.

"This was the first intimation I had of her being married—and though I recoiled at the idea of concealment, yet the injury that I might have done the woman, who had hazarded much for me, overcame my repugnance, and I suffered myself to be immured in a closet. I was pretty quiet for a few minutes—but my impatience at my confinement, (for I have but a small stock of that virtue) irritated me, and I began to pace the closet, in agitation, when my foot, coming in contact with a stand of flowers, threw them down, and created a tremendous crash. I soon heard voices, in loud altercation, advancing to the closet. There was a window in it, and I, to save the lady's reputation, leaped out of it, sealed the wall, and got clear off— chagrined at my disappointment, early next day I planted myself opposite the house, and was joined by the duenna, who told me to be at the garden-gate at the same hour as on the night before, and she would be there to receive me. Returning to the city, I called on my banker, and related to him the last evening's adventure, concealing nothing but the lady's name and abode—which he seemed desirous to know.

"Curse on the meddling fool of a husband! said I, for interrupting me, when I was about to decorate his brows in such a manner that he should have rivaled Actæon in the beauty of his antlers. But, he shall pay for all to-night.

"I was at my rendezvous, at the appointed time, and

was conducted to the same chamber as before—where the considerate duenna left me, *tête-à-tête*, with my charmer. I pressed my suit with ardour, and my condescending mistress seemed ready to bless my wishes, when my evil genius again interposed. The cursed bell was rung, with a most infernal clamour, and Ursula burst into the room, vociferating—

'Jesu Maria! there is my master again!'

"I knew not what to do: the closet had been so unfortunate before, that I exclaimed against concealing myself there—nor indeed, would it have been prudent—having learned that the enraged husband had searched it, after my escape (which he was led to do by the cursed clatter I had made) and finding the stand thrown down, and the window open, it was not without much trouble that they lulled his jealous suspicions.

"In this dilemma, it was proposed by Ursula, that she should open the gate, and extinguish the light at the same moment; and that I should slip out, as her master entered —which plan was agreed to, and happily executed.

"Hearing the duenna at high words with her master, I tarried at the gate till the cry of murder from within, drew the neighbours to the spot—and Ursula coming to the door of perturbation, a group of them entered the house. Among the rest I went in—but, how shall I express my amazement when in the person of the enraged husband (who was cudgelling his wife) I saw my little banker! the contriver of the plot—against himself! As soon as he espied me, he grinned like an enraged baboon, and cried:

'That's the thief! that's the plunderer of my honour! Oh! you villain! have you not made me the tool of my own shame? have not you made me commit murder—the murder of my own happiness?—While I thought I was only stabbing at the peace of another, I was cutting my own throat—and all through your hellish artifices!'

"The mob conceived the word *murder* according to its *literal* acceptation, and vociferated—'A lunatic! a lunatic!'

'No, no—I am no lunatic, but an ill-used man,' quoth he. 'In the devil's name! what business had that old Jezabel to take her to mass?—A plague on those pampered monks, and all belonging to 'em!—They are the progenitors of all intrigue and wickedness—and a man may as well send his wife to a stew as to where they are.'

'A heretic! a heretic!' roared his auditors.

'I am no heretic, but a true church-going Catholic, good people,' replied he, alarmed at their last assertion. 'But, I have been grossly abused—and if I were to go mad, that villain would have it to answer for.'

"With a provoking coolness, and insulting pity, I told him, though I never had had the pleasure of seeing him before, I was concerned for his misfortune: that I believed he was moon-stricken and would recommend clean straw and a little bread and water, as the only means of restoring his senses.

"The mob proceeded to lay hands on him—at which, being no longer able to refrain from laughing, I hastened off. I made several attempts to gain another interview, but the old rogue had removed his rib—and (going to Ireland soon after, to visit my family) I have never seen her since.

"Such, gentlemen, is the story I promised you, and which finishes with our journey—for these are the gates of Seville."

CHAP. II.

Ah! me! for aught that ever I could read,
Could ever hear, by tale or history,
The course of true love never did run smooth—

A MIDSUMMER NIGHT'S DREAM.[1]

RODORIGO's rank gave him and his party access to the first circles—and among others, to the Duke of Murcia—a nobleman who had lately fixed his residence at Seville.

The duke was a widower, with a son and two daughters; the younger of whom (agreeable to the policy of Catholic countries) was designed for the cloister, while her brother and sister were to enjoy the splendid inheritance of their ancestors.—The young marquis was married, and resided at Burgos, but the daughters remained with their father, who was a strict observer of the rules prescribed by the church of Rome, and an inveterate enemy to every thing heretical.

The day following the arrival of the travellers, they attended a splendid *fête* at the duke's palace, given by him in honour of his elder daughter's natal day—and were introduced to the ladies.

Elvira's features were beautiful—but the fulness of her dark eye had an effect of boldness, and her air was more commanding than conciliating: while her younger sister Angela (like the sensitive plant) seemed to shrink from the admiration she excited, and the emanation of her blue eyes beamed diffidence and benignity so sweetly blended,

1 1.1.132-134.

94

that Lord Liffey, at his first interview, became her devoted slave. Not as he had before pledged himself to the banker's wife—that was a casual amour, on which he entered with all the extravagance of spirit that characterizes his countrymen—but this was founded on reason and principle, and his only wish was to make the lovely Angela his bride.

Among various sports and exercises, the duke proclaimed a bull-feast, and gave a general invitation to all cavaliers, who chose to try their prowess[1]—and as an incitement to the brave, prizes were to be bestowed by their fair hands of the sisters, on the two champions, who should be adjudged to have exhibited most proofs of valour. A large circle was formed in front of the palace, with seats for the spectators, and in one part a throne was elevated, covered with cloth of gold, for the reception of the duke and his family—and there, amid the clash of martial music, they took their seats.

Several bulls were let loose, and various proofs of courage and agility, evinced by their opponents. At last, a huge black animal (whose blood-shot eyes struck terror) appeared, and made the amphitheatre shake with his bellowings. At sight of him, Lord Liffey entered the lists—and while others pricked the bull with small darts behind, he irritated him in front to the combat. The furious animal driven mad by goading, tore up the earth, and made several desperate plunges at his antagonist, which he artfully evaded—until the animal unfortunately struck his curved horns into the horse's side, and threw him and his rider to the ground together. He was now about to repeat his advantage; when the Irishman disengaging himself from his steed, and seizing the horns of the enraged bull, vaulted with wonderful address upon his back, and lodged

---

1 'process' in the first edition, an apparent error.

his spear in the spinal marrow of the beast. With an hideous roar he sunk beneath his conqueror, in whose praise the shouts of the spectators rent the air.

Being adjudged victor, together with a descendant of the noble house of Medina, he approached the throne, whereon the sisters sat—but instead of stopping for the glittering reward of a chaplet of Orient pearls, tendered by Elvira, he gracefully bowed, past on to her lovely sister, and kneeling, received a white scarf, with silver roses, worked by her own hand—and which he prized before the boasted gems of Golconda.

This indifference wounded the haughty Elvira, whose pride had *condescended* to regard him with no unfavourable eye; and she now wished to think with contempt of a man who could pay homage to the *insipid* charms of her sister, to the prejudice of her own *dazzling* beauty. This mortification was heightened by the evident assiduity with which he plied the gentle Angela, during the remainder of the entertainment, and she retired at night full of spleen.

"You look very heavy and out of spirits, my lady," observed her waiting maid. "How can you, for whom all our dons are dying, and would give the world for the slightest token of your favour, be so?"

"You are mistaken," said Elvira, with acrimony: "I have been treated with disdain—and the only man who ever made any impression on my heart, slights the conquest, and prefers my *automaton* sister."

"Oh! the virgin! is it possible there should be a man so blind!—May your humble servant, Signora—take the liberty to ask the name of this insensible?"

"You saw him to-day—the handsome young foreigner, who was introduced by Don Rodorigo de Henares."

"Handsome, lady?" rejoined the waiting-woman.—"You have had thousands of suitors that he is not fit to hold a candle to—and I am sure, your beauty may command thousands more."

"Hold!" cried Elvira: "though he has insulted me, and lowered me in my own opinion, I still think him superior to all the men I ever saw."

"Certainly, Signora, I must confess he is handsome enough—and you would make a most charming couple," said the accommodating servant. "But, if your ladyship is smitten (pardon my boldness!) there are ways and means of getting your sister out of the way. You know, my lord, your father, is very suspicious—and a *gentle hint* (though but for your sake my lady, I would sooner die than utter an untruth) would remove her at once. You know, it would only be the means of her being sent to a monastery a little sooner than she would otherwise have been—and she ought to thank your ladyship for hurrying her away from this world of temptation."

How far Elvira profited by this advice will be quickly seen.

Lord Liffey (at his next visit) learned, to his extreme chagrin, that his adored Angela had been conveyed to a convent that morning, and was to enter on her novitiate without delay. He had heard from Rodorigo that she was destined to a monastic life—but his sanguine mind anticipated the pleasure of frustrating the unjust scheme of the duke, and of bearing away so lovely a prize to grace his paternal board. Here, then, his plan was marred: but Liffey's love was as persevering as sincere, and after the first pangs of disappointment, he meditated the idea of discovering where she was immured, and of possessing her, in spite of monastic vigilance, and all other obstacles. To aim at deriving any intelligence from the duke would, he knew, be fruitless—as the little he had seen of him served to shew the reserve of his character—and our lover fancied himself treated at this visit with coolness. Nevertheless, he entertained hopes of being enabled to corrupt some of the servants with his gold—and in this instance, he deemed such a step justifiable.

He made his parting obeisance to the duke, with a distant air; and as buried in meditation, he crossed the hall, he saw a female wringing her hands, and crying bitterly—

"That her dear young lady, her sweet Donna Angela, was taken from her!"

"Ha! fortune! thou seem'st to be propitious!" thought Liffey—and in passing her, he whispered: "If your lady *is* dear to you, follow me. I will wait for you, in the great square."

There he was joined by the female; who told him (with tears in her eyes) that she had been Donna Angela's waiting-woman since they were both fourteen years of age.

"Indeed, Signor, it is very hard to be separated, after three years faithful service," continued she: "for I would have served her still, for nothing. And don't you think it a *mortal* shame, Signor, to lock up a beautiful young lady, like her, in an odious nunnery?"

"I do indeed!" replied Liffey: "and if you can direct me to the place of her confinement, I will release her at the hazard of my life; and you shall remain with her, till the end of your's."

"As sure as can be, you are some saint come to give me comfort!" quoth the girl, her countenance brightening. "No, no; I am wrong: you are the cavalier that my lady told me she gave the scarf to, at the bull-feast. Are you not?"

"The same," answered Liffey. "But, tell me—did she speak kindly of me?"

"A great deal more so than I shall let you know," rejoined the artless wench: "because, you men, when once you know a woman loves you, grow careless; and you may give up the thought of getting my lady out of that nasty nunnery, perhaps, if I was to tell you all."

"Do not fear that.—By all my hopes I will never cease, till I've released her!"

"Won't you?—Heaven bless you, Signor! you shall know all. The day after the bull-feast, Donna Angela took her morning walk, and I with her. As we went on—talking about one thing or another—'Did you see the bull-feast, yesterday?' said she.—No, my lady says I.—'I wish *I* had not!' says she, with a sigh.—Why so, my lady? says I.—'Because, the cavalier who took my prize, rather than my sister's, took my heart at the same time. He is the only man I ever saw, that made me think of a convent with dislike —and if I had my choice, I would pass my life in a cottage with him, rather than live in a palace without him,' says she.—Now, Signor, what say you?"

"Say!" exclaimed he. "That you have made me the happiest man in the world. But where is the lovely Angela confined?"

"I don't know, Signor."

"Not know?" repeated he, in a tone of disappointment.

"No, Signor: I did hear about three months ago, that Donna Angela was to take the veil in the convent of Saint Mary, here, in the city; but I don't know whether she is there or not."

"That I will soon ascertain," said the lover. "In the mean time, take this purse, as an earnest of my wish to serve you, and tell me where I may see you again."

"You will find me, Signor, at my brother's—Lazarillo, a shoemaker, adjoining the wall of the monastery of Saint Benedict," said she; "and I shall be very happy to hear of my dear mistress, and to assist her all in my power. As to your gold you must excuse me, Signor: my affection can't be made greater by that, and I scorn to be paid for performing my duty."

It was to no purpose he pressed her to take the purse; she persisted in her refusal, and they separated—he, to the convent of Saint Mary, for tidings of his Angela, and she to the shoemaker's, to wait his return.

In the evening, a knocking was heard at the door of honest Lazarillo; and Flora, his sister, opened it to an emaciated lame wretch, with a hump-back, and one eye covered with a black patch.

"Is this the house of Master Lazarillo?" demanded he, in a feeble lisp.

"It is.—What is your business with him, friend?" said she.

"My business is with his sister."

"I am his sister," replied Flora.

"Are you so? Well, I am come to tell you, I know where your lady Donna Angela is confined; and if you think she would be so grateful as to marry me, I would undertake to set her at liberty."

"You, you ugly monster!" cried Flora—"my sweet young mistress marry you?—She would sooner die where she is!"

"Nay, but hear me," lisped the man. "I am not so poor as you may think—I have a thousand crowns in gold; and that, and giving her liberty, ought to command something."

"If you had the riches of India, my lady would not listen to you," vociferated the enraged Flora. "But, be packing, or my brother shall lay the stirrup-leather about your back: go, or every shoe in the shop shall go at your head!"

She turned her back upon the stranger, and was walking to the other end of the shop, in violent anger, when she heard him burst into a hearty laugh; and turning to reprimand him, she saw the supposed cripple had thrown off his patch, and black hair, and was no other than Lord Liffey!

"Forgive me, my dear Flora, for the rage I have put you in!" said he. "But my disguise is not to end here—since you did not discover me under it, I shall set about my scheme with a double assurance of success."

"Lord, Signor," replied she—"the devil himself could not have known you. But what of my lady?"

"He informed her briefly, that when he left her, he went to a tavern, opposite the great gate of the convent—the master of which he knew, and hoped to gain information from. That, when he was taking his wine, and conversing with his host, a servant informed the latter, father Peccadillo desired to see him—on which he apologized to his lordship, and promised to return as soon as he had dispatched the monk, who was confessor to the opposite convent. Liffey, for a very obvious reason, desired to be introduced to his reverence—to which, the landlord assented—saying, the old monk was a good-natured soul, and took a glass as freely as any one.

"The father was ushered into the room—and after some casual talk, the host began to joke his reverence, on the late addition to the community of Saint Mary—affirming that the most beautiful creature he had ever seen was brought to the convent that morning. Father Peccadillo said he had heard she was a most delectable creature: that she was the daughter of one of the first grandees, and was to enter on her novitiate sooner than had been intended, to avoid the addresses of a needy foreign adventurer.

'But,' pursued the priest, 'to the business that I came to you upon. Their gardener at the convent is dead—and as they are much in want of one to fill his place, if you can recommend such a one, you will oblige the lady abbess.'

"Not a syllable of this was lost on me," continued Lord Liffey—"and without hesitation, I acquainted the friar that I knew of a gardener, on whom I would place as much dependence as on *myself*—and for whose fidelity I should not hesitate to become bound—if he thought he could rely on the recommendation of a stranger as I was to him. To this my host observed that he would guarantee anything I promised, and it was settled that I should send my gardener to-morrow.

"Accordingly I sent and purchased these clothes, with an idea of imposing myself on the convent, as the person I had recommended—and (as I said) I called on you to ascertain whether it was likely my disguise would answer my purpose."

Here he closed his account—and said, if he should be so fortunate as to carry his point, he would not fail to give Flora such intimation as should enable her to join her mistress—and (if she thought fit) of accompanying her to a distant country. To this proposal, Flora replied, she was willing to follow her to the end of the world.

A second knocking at the door was answered by Flora, and a man inquired for Lord Liffey. This was Murdoch, who had been ordered to join his master there, and who, on seeing him so curiously equipt, said, he put him in mind of *ould* Clinterduffy, the *game*-legged piper of Wexford. His master gave him some instructions, and departed, with the good wishes of the two humble but honest creatures he left behind.

A week elapsed, from the time Lord Liffey entered on his low occupation, without his having seen Angela, although he had scrutinized the figures of the sisterhood, as they took their walk in the garden, and he almost began to despair; when he had the pleasure to see her with one of the nuns enter the alley wherein he was employed. He had a letter ready for the occasion, and he found means to deliver it to her, unperceived by her companion. In it he informed her who he was, and what was his design—and conjured her, if the window of her cell looked on to the garden, to drop a note from it at eleven o'clock that night —when he would be on the watch. He concluded with an exhortation to her, to support her spirits—and to rely on him who was ready to sacrifice his life in attempting to restore her to freedom.

The lady returned her answer—and in an ingenuous[1] manner confessed there was no man to whom she would so soon owe her liberation, as himself. Liffey almost devoured the billet with kisses—and perceiving the window was not very high, he contrived (with the assistance of a mulberry-tree that grew beneath) to climb it —and beheld his mistress within, perusing a letter; which he rightly judged to be his own. Angela started when he tapped gently on the glass—but a repetition led her to the window, where she found her lover. Fearful of discovery, he proceeded to say, that if she would authorize him, he would provide the means for her escape, against the next night but one, and conduct her to a country where, if she would condescend to unite her destiny to his, each hour of his life should be devoted to her. Suffice it to say, her answer was such as made him happy—and now (however strong his inclination to enjoy the society of his mistress a few minutes longer) he appointed the hour of eleven for their departure, and tore himself from her.

Under pretext of purchasing plants, he went out, on the following day, and called at the house of Lazarillo (where Murdoch had taken up his lodging) and bade him and Flora hold themselves in readiness to leave Spain, and be

[1] In the first edition, 'ingenious'.

under the south wall of the convent-garden at eleven next night, where he would meet them. He purchased a ladder of ropes, which he concealed in a sack, and then returned to the convent.

The interval of time he spent in scooping vacancies in the cement of the stonework to enable him to climb the wall. At length, the wished-for hour arrived: three taps at Angela's window was the signal, which she answered by opening the casement—the ladder was fixed to the window, and with her lover's assistance she descended.

With cautious steps they approached the wall, which Liffey with little difficulty scaled, had fixed the grapples, and was about to return for his beloved companion, when four men rushed from an arbour, and rudely seized her. Transported with rage and disappointment, to be wrecked as it were in sight of port, the undaunted lover unsheathed his sword, and threw himself from the wall, into the midst of the unknown intruders.

CHAP. III.

Remorseless, treacherous, leacherous, kindless villain!

HAMLET.[1]

DURING the absence of Lord Liffey (for which Rodorigo could not account) a letter was delivered to the latter, from old Lewis; adjuring him if he wished to see the Count before he died, to lose no time in setting off for the castle: as Don Hannibal had quitted it—and the old nobleman had no relative to attend his sick bedside, save his niece Aurora, who was as much in want of some friend to console her, as himself.

1 2.2.558.

"There is little chance of his dying, I believe," said Rodo-rigo, mentally.—"These tedious old fools live for ever; or at least, till they wear their heirs' expectations into the wane.—I will go—and heaven send, before I reach him, the dotard may sleep on the bosom of Abraham!—or any where else, so as he is out of my way!"

On entering his paternal roof, he was accosted by Lewis.

"How is my father?" demanded the dissembler. "I am worn with the speed I have made to wait on him—and I trust he is as I wish him."

"Faith, Signor, that I cannot say," replied the steward; "but he is very bad."

"Worse than when you wrote?"

"Much worse."

"Then he is in great danger, I suppose?" cried Rodo-rigo, hardly able to dissemble his joy. "But I hope he will recover."

"I hope he will!" quoth Lewis. "But as you have so fatigued yourself in hurrying to your sick father, 'tis a pity you should now lose any time in going to him, Signor.— Jesu preserve him! for if he should die, heaven knows where we should get such another master!"

The young lord cast on him a look of contempt, and muttered—"Indeed!"—He then passed on to the Count's apartment: who was fast asleep, and at the instant of Rodorigo's entrance, he cried:

"Torrismond! Torrismond! my dear Torrismond!"

"Damnation!" said Rodorigo to himself—"even in his dreams that libertine is his chief care!—But I must disturb your sweet dreams: these slumbers may refresh you, and you may still stand between me and fortune.—Wake my dear father, wake!" concluded he.

The sight of his son appeared to revive the old noble-man; he raised himself on the pillow, and folding him in his arms, wept upon his neck—while the crocodile tears of the other, (for he had them at command) were mingled with his parent's.

"My Rodorigo! my dear boy!" said the count, in a broken voice, "thou art come in time to close my eyes, and I shall die in peace."

"Oh! do not talk of dying, my beloved parent!" exclaimed the hypocrite, "unless you wish to cleave the heart of your son!—I have posted to you on the wings of duty; and doubt not, but you will live many happy years to bless me."

"Heaven bless you!" returned the count. "But indeed my dear son, I cannot survive long. Oh! had I now thy brother with me—were he here to receive my dying bless-ing—I should be content indeed!"

The wily son poured forth a torrent of affectionate and dutiful expressions—and concluded with a prayer that he would endeavour to compose himself to rest.

Rodorigo had been at home five days, and the count seemed approaching towards convalescence, when the castle was one night alarmed by the cries of the former (who had sat up with his father) and many of the family rushed into the room—where they found the old man in strong convulsions—which terminated his existence in a few hours.

In the general lamentation, none was more *clamorous* than Rodorigo—he tore his hair, beat his forehead, and exhibited all the symptoms of violent grief. Aurora's was a deep, an heart-felt sorrow—that found no vent in words—but like the canker-worm, was feeding on her vitals. Lewis, the faithful Lewis, offered a prayer to heaven, to avert the ills he dreaded:

"Here will be a dismal change," said he. "Santa Maria protect them who are under Signor Rodorigo's power!—

Ah! poor Don Torrismond! my dear young master! had *you* remained to fill the place of your worthy father, it would have been some consolation!—Well, well, heaven's will be done!"

At these words he dashed away the tears which streamed through the time-worn channels of his cheeks, and prostrated himself before his favourite saint.

The remains of the count were conveyed to the monastery of Saint Augustine, to be deposited with those of his ancestors—and there was not one of his dependents, but dropt a tear to his remembrance.

Don Rodorigo no longer sought concealment of his vices, beneath the specious gloss of virtue. For be it known, his former apparent coldness of disposition was not the effect of nature, but of art.—He possessed every vicious passion that can disgrace human nature, but he had hitherto made them subservient to his interests—and the removal of certain barriers, which had stood between him, and the family title and estates, had called forth the whole stock of his consummate dissimulation. That obstacle being removed, he set the opinion of the world (which lately was his aim to obtain) at defiance—and stood confessed—

A bold-faced villain!

He entered Aurora's chamber, one afternoon, and found her in tears.[1]

"Retired already, fair mourner?" said he.—"Why have you stolen from me, and marred the conviviality I hoped to have enjoyed in your society?"

"For shame, my lord! I blush to hear you.—The solemn

1 In the original text, Palmer refers to Aurora here as Angela, the maiden pursued by Lord Liffey. As it is clear that Rodorigo is speaking to Aurora, and not Angela, as this conversation continues, I have corrected the character's name here.

death-bell which tolled thy father to his grave, is still sounding in our ears, and the black banner waves on the battlements, yet canst thou talk of conviviality!"

"Mean you then to weep for ever?—The dead sleep in peace: leave them to enjoy their repose, and make the living happy. On you, and you alone, depends the happiness of Rodorigo. You know my passion, and it is now time you should repay it."

"That, my lord," replied she, "it will *never* be. Were your proffered love such as inclination would bid me listen to, at another time, the indelicacy of the addresses with which you have lately *tormented* me (since the loss of your revered father) would prevent my regarding you with any other sentiment than that of indignation."

"Romantic enthusiast!" cried Rodorigo, "know'st thou not the uncertainty of man's life?—None but fools procrastinate their bliss—and then mourn the folly of delay. But say—if I should defer my suit for awhile, will you in proper season requite my love?"

"My lord," returned Aurora firmly, "I have not learned your happy art of dissimulation—and 'tis my honesty of nature which tells you, I never will be your's. My heart *was* devoted to another: he proved unworthy, and it shall never be given again—and last of all to you. With the fortune my honoured uncle left me, I will retire from the world: a cloister is the sanctuary for disappointed love, and within one, the wretched Aurora means to end her days. For you, my lord! your disrespect to the best of fathers, in insulting his ashes with unseemly levity, demands an age of penitence. But if your heart has room for love, go to the marchioness, go to the wronged Philippa. (Ah! dost thou change?)—Yes, she has disclosed her injuries—and if thou hast any hope of mercy, when thou shalt want it most, make reparation, and heal her bleeding wounds!"

With a look of mingled contempt and pity, she left him, unable to prevent her retreat. That Philippa should have betrayed their mutual intercourse to his cousin, and complained of the wrongs he had done her, was so inconsistent with her excessive pride, that the knowledge of it rivetted him to the spot.

After a short rumination, he meditated a project that would, if it succeeded, put him in possession of the person of Aurora—which done, he was to wreak his vengeance on the chattering Philippa. Not that he heeded the rumour of his amour with her being published—for he had divested himself of all regard for the world's censures—and he well knew she would (for her own sake) conceal the *only* circumstance that could affect him.

His plan arranged, he walked to the cottage of Volponé (the ruffian with whom he held the dialogue partly overheard by Lewis) situated at the distance of a league from Henares castle. The owner was at home, and Rodorigo opened his purpose to him without reserve. He told him to go to the castle in disguise, and to ask to speak with Donna Aurora. He was to impose himself on her, as a messenger from Carlos, who (he was to say) was waiting at the cottage, and humbly implored, in the name of their past loves, to see her there that evening. That he was innocent of the murder of Don Hilario (however circumstances might militate against him) and if she would deign to grant him the interview, he did not doubt, but he should be able to *convince* her he was not guilty. Such was the purport of the message—and if she consented to visit the cottage, the owner was to absent himself at the time, and the dæmon, Rodorigo, was to fill the place of the expected Carlos.

Having given him his instructions, and promised an immense reward, he exhorted his emissary to be particular. Volponé bade him not to fear: for that he would sooner be whipt barefooted through hell, than not obey an employer who promised so generously.

Happy that his scheme was in so fair a train, Rodorigo departed—and as he measured back his steps, fell into the following reflection.

"What a world is this?—How impetuously that rascal enters into my schemes, in the hope of a reward, that were he not insane, he must be convinced he will never obtain!—Can he expect me to fulfil my promise, which would strike at the root of one third of my possessions?— Oh! it is unpardonable!—This slave is a villain to the heart's core—yet he trusts to the promises of another. *He will be whipt through hell, rather than not obey an employer, who promises so generously.* The fool goes forth to betray an innocent woman; and yet, when he finds he has been duped, himself, he will never forgive. If such wretches are the boasted lords of the creation, I stand excused for waging eternal war against them."

The next day, Rodorigo was convinced his emissary had been as good as his word, Aurora's agitation during dinner, being such, as she could not totally disguise—and he applied the goblet to his lips, that by the appointed time, he was half intoxicated.

It was just after the close of day that Rodorigo set out for the cottage of Volponé, anticipating the disappointment of his cousin, when she should behold him instead of Carlos. He raised the latch of the door, and beheld (by the aid of a melancholy and uncertain light, which the moon just risen, shed through a misty atmosphere) a female within—whom he thus addressed:—

"Am I so happy as to meet you here?—By Saint Antony 'tis more than I promised myself! But doubly should I estimate the blessing, did I not know, the hope of seeing another led you hither. How then shall the detested Rodorigo apologize," demanded he, in an ironical accent, "for obtruding himself into the presence of her who anticipated the pleasure of a meeting with Don Carlos—the amiable and adored?"

Obtaining no answer, he resumed.

"Am I to interpret your taciturnity into a *fixed* aversion, or has circumstance lowered your imperious tone?—Yes, haughty damsel!—I will now enjoy that by force, for which I lately pleaded in vain—and without galling myself with the detestable chains of matrimony. My wife! no, you shall not have that honour: you shall be my mistress awhile—and when satiety shall have dulled the keen edge of desire, I will expose you to the taunts of our peasants' wives, who shall point at you, as you pass them.—The indignation you yesterday expressed against me, for deserting the foolish marchioness, would have been well reserved for your own unhappy state—such as I shall leave you in.—Come, I will defer my purpose no longer: your resistance will adorn my triumph, and season my voluptuousness."

As he advanced to accomplish his fell design, the female threw off her veil, and the voice of the marchioness exclaimed: "Villain! deliberate villain! have I found thee!—Was it not enough that my honour, innocence, and peace of mind, have been devoted to thee, but thou must hold me up (as was thy thought) to the derision of a third person?—Know thou, all-sapient miscreant! the *foolish* Philippa is not to be insulted with impunity."

"I have gone too far to recede," replied Rodorigo, with an insulting coldness;—"and I will now (for the first time) deal candidly with you. You have been liberal in your favours to me, and I *was* thankful. But love, and all engagements, have an end, when interest, or caprice demands the dissolution. We are no children, Philippa! then listen to the voice of reason. I here cancel the bond of faith you pledged to me, and more, advise you to seek that love from another, which I have not longer the power to bestow on you. As to my own vows, I ask for no release from them—for at the time I made them, 'twas with a resolve no longer to observe their purport, than might suit my own convenience."

"Eternal Ruler!" cried the marchioness, half choaked with contending emotions, "hast thou no bolt, red with uncommon vengeance, to hurl against this monster—who ridicules the oaths registered in thy never-failing memory?"

"Stop!" interrupted Rodorigo: "if oaths are *sacred* things, what punishment awaits them, who violate the *marriage*-vow, and riot in adultery? Is there no bolt reserved for one, who with a subtle poison, sends her husband *prematurely* to his grave?"

"I feel the guilt more, at this moment, than I e'er did before; when such a wretch as thou, who luredst me to the crime, darst to reproach me with the sin entailed upon it. But hear me—power supreme! and, oh, let not my own guilt hang heavy on my prayer, and clog its flight!—Whate'er it be thy will *I* suffer—suffer I will with patience—but oh! God! strike that wretch with present affliction, and be his torments hereafter without end!"

"Reserve your curses! for on me they are lost," returned the hardened wretch. "Possessed of fortune, I bid defiance to affliction *here*, and for *hereafter*, let churchmen fright the foolish and the fearful—I laugh, to scorn, their precepts and their threats!"

"Indeed!" exclaimed Philippa. "I'll try this boasted bravery—and, whate'er may be my own disgrace, I will proclaim the villainy to the world. I go, to prove my words."

"Hold! you would not think of exposing me."——

"Is there *no* way to avert the publication of my conduct?" demanded Rodorigo, with a sneer.

"None: the prayers of angels should not move me," replied she.

"Stay! I have yet one argument to use in my behalf—a strong one—and, *may it touch thy heart!*" cried the sanguinary villain, drawing his dagger, and plunging it in her bosom.

She fell—and as the livid hue of death spread itself over her fine features, she faltered out this prophetic speech.

"'Tis done! providence is just! I receive my death-wound from the monster to whom I sacrificed my all, and my sins are (I trust) washed away in my blood.—For thee! the measure of thy crimes is nearly full, and the sword of an offended Deity now trembles o'er thee!—Even now, methinks I see a thousand hideous furies dance around thee, and point at thee, as their destined prey! Whate'er thy atheistical mind may deem my words, of this be sure —a dreadful death awaits thee in this world (and most like) a life of eternal torture, in the next!—Repent and strive to save thy soul!—if it be not too late!"——

She groaned and died.

The conscience-stricken Rodorigo, gazing on the work of his fell hand, and fancying fiends really surrounded him, thus broke the awful silence:

"What have I done?—Is there a world to come?—If it be so, I am lost, past all redemption. I am too deeply damned to hope for pardon. Pardon for such hell-born crimes as mine! can I expect it?—oh! never! never!"

"*Never!*" repeated a voice, in a deep emphatic accent.

The murderer stood aghast—for the tone resembled that of his father. Terror awhile suspended his power of speech, and every limb trembled. At length, he endeavoured to rally his scattered senses, and exclaimed:

"If thou art of mortal substance, who in this dreary spot and silent hour, wrapt in deep mystery, hast shaken my manhood to the centre, I charge thee to appear, and meet me point to point! If my soul flinch from the encounter, may I be cursed for ever!"

"*Be cursed for ever!*" echoed the same mysterious voice.

If Rodorigo before entertained any doubt of its being the voice of his departed sire, it was now banished—for the tones carried conviction to his heart. He staggered to the door, and having past the threshold, fled to the castle with all the speed he was master of—nor turned his head till he had crossed the drawbridge, lest his eyes should encounter the spirit of his dead parent.

He locked himself in his chamber, and it was some time before he could arrange his ideas, so as to account, in any probable way, for the appearance of the marchioness, in lieu of Aurora. One minute he suspected Volponé had betrayed him—but the knowledge he had of the ruffian's avarice removed that apprehension from his mind—which was presently occupied by a surmise, that Aurora, suspecting some deception, had opened her mind to Philippa; and that the latter, no stranger to his artifices, had deemed him the contriver of it, and taken the place of his intended victim, in order to reproach him with his infidelity.

"Be that as it may," concluded he; "the curious Philippa has paid the price of her intrusion; and since I have bought this haughty fair with blood, she shall be mine—though hell stood yawning to oppose my purpose!"

He swallowed a goblet of wine, and went to Aurora's apartment—but no Aurora was there. He summoned his people, and ordered them to search every avenue of the castle—but all was fruitless—she was not to be found.— The unhallowed execrations of the disappointed villain were heard on all sides: he cursed Aurora and those who had connived at her escape; and sent out emissaries in pursuit of her—with this caution:—

"If they valued their lives, not to return without her."

Meanwhile, Aurora (who had intimation of his villainous designs, by means not necessary to be elucidated at present) quitted the castle in the dusk of evening, clad in pilgrims' weeds. As she pursued her fearful way, she ever and anon averted her head, and cast a wistful glance at the mansion of her youth—while a sigh would escape her tortured bosom, and a tear steal down her lily cheek, at the remembrance of the many happy days she had past there—never to return.

"It was a fine calm evening," said she, as she paused in reverie—"the last but one before Carlos departed from Henares, when he took me into yonder grove, where oft we used to sit together, absorbed in dreams of love.—We remained long silent: at length he grasped my hand, and said softly to me, with tears in his eyes:—

'Soon do I leave you, Aurora—I know not why, but my mind forebodes that it will be for ever.—Should my fears be prophetic, do not forget me—do not too hastily pledge your faith to another, should Carlos—never—return!'—

"I swore my faith should never be plighted to another—and heaven forget me, when I forget my vow!"

She journeyed on till day-break, when the barking of a dog convinced her she was near some habitation; and as the light increased, she saw smoke issue from above a copse of fig-trees. She made for the spot, and passing through a gate, entered a serpentine walk, at the end whereof was a neat cottage, standing in the midst of a grass-plot, planted with roses, jessamines, honeysuckles, and other odoriferous flowers.

An old woman was attending her bee-hives, and a young one was watering the flowers. Perceiving our pilgrim, the latter approached; when observing that she looked pale and faint, she threw away the machine, and called her mother to assist in taking the stranger into the house.

They set before her fruit and goat's milk—of which they both (addressing her by the appellation of "good youth,") begged her to partake, and which much recruited her strength. She was delighted with the native simplicity and good nature of Rosa, her young entertainer, but there was a reserve about her old hostess that chilled her. After her repast, she retired to a bed, where the downy poppies of Morpheus closed her eyes and the black prospect of retrospection and futurity were for a time excluded.

Night had spread her sable mantle o'er the earth, when our fugitive, with a thankful heart, bade adieu to her hostesses; to each of them she presented a token of remembrance, and received from Rosa a bouquet of roses, which as she gave, she moistened with her tears—for the supposed pilgrim had made an impression of a very tender nature upon her young heart.

The air was serene, and the moon rose[1] in a fine, clear sky, when Aurora departed; but she had journeyed only a short distance, when the face of the atmosphere became condense; the wind whistled, and the flying clouds obscured the planet of night, which lent an intermitting light, hardly sufficient to enable her to shun the bogs and precipices, which she was liable to meet with.

It was by the side of a clump of cork-trees, whose boughs waved mournfully, that the sight of a white object attracted her attention, and she advanced to it. It was a stone tablet—and Aurora with some difficulty deciphered the following inscription:

1 In the first edition, 'rode'.

"This Stone
was placed here,
In Commemoration
of a most
Inhuman Murder!
committed by a gang of
Freebooters,
who have long infested
These Mountains,
to the terror of all
Passengers.
Justice
however, has overtaken
Three of the Assassins;
who have atoned."——

A creaking noise prevented her proceeding. Trembling with terror, she turned her eyes towards the heath, and they encountered the view of a triangular gibbet—on which were suspended the bodies of three men, whose chains grated in the night-breeze!

She was almost overcome with terror, at these concurring horrors—her knees smote each other in dreadful trepidation, and cold drops stood upon her forehead. With much difficulty she moved onward—when she found her way obstructed by a chasm, through which a rapid stream of water rushed, whose hoarse roaring increased the awfulness of night.—The trunk of a beech-tree was thrown across, for the accommodation of passengers—and with tottering steps, the fair fugitive attempted to pass it—but she had hardly gained the middle, when her foot slipt, and she fell into the roaring stream beneath!

CHAP. IV.

None but the brave deserve the fair!

ALEXANDER'S FEAST.[1]

LORD Liffey (whom we left engaged with the men, that seized Angela, in the convent-garden) withstood their united attacks, till, overpowered by numbers, he was disarmed, bound, and cast into a dungeon.[2] The subsequent morning, he was taken before the corrigidor, upon the charge of having attempted to steal a novice—and it is most likely, his adventure would have had a serious termination, had he not fortunately been recognized by the magistrate—to whom he was known, during his last stay in Spain.

The corrigidor begged him to favour him with a candid recital of the affair, and in return, pledged himself to exert every effort his situation, both as a friend and a magistrate, would allow to rescue him from the impending danger. Thus adjured, Liffey related the transaction and finished with a vow, that should he recover his liberty, he would take no rest till he had accomplished his purpose.

The good-natured magistrate requested him to be patient, and sent him to solicit the attendance of the Duke of Murcia at his house. When he arrived, and was examined, as to the charge preferred against Liffey, he deposed—that it had always been his determination, that

1 John Dryden (1631-1700), "Alexander's Feast" (1697), 15.
2 In the original text, Palmer again confused his female characters, naming Aurora here instead of Angela.

his younger daughter should take the veil—and that the introduction of the prisoner to his family had accelerated the accomplishment of it. He had accordingly removed Donna Angela to a monastery, from which place the prisoner (in defiance of religion) had attempted to convey her—and he demanded justice for the sacrilege.

"I hope your lordship will pardon the liberty I am about to take," said the corrigidor—"but what objection can you have to uniting your daughter to a man, who is every way your lordship's equal?"

"Were I not so well convinced of your integrity, I should suppose you were in league with my enemy," replied the duke. "But I will inform your lordship of the reasons for my invincible objections to the measure. In the first place, this foreigner is an heretic (that is an insuperable bar) and secondly, he is an adventurer, affecting kindred to nobility while his blood, in reality, is of the lowest order."

"If your lordship's first position is founded on no surer basis than the last, I am convinced I shall be able to refute the gross aspersion thrown on the character of this young nobleman. I know him to be the son of the Earl of Leinster —a baron whom his country boasts none more ancient or honourable, and I think I know him well enough to contradict the infamous accusation of his having renounced the religion of his ancestors."

"My lord," said Liffey, who had not before interrupted the conversation, "as I can prove I am no other than the man for whom I have passed myself upon you—I expect that you will reveal to me the name of my asperser, that I may exact from him such satisfaction as the laws of injured honour intitle me to—for I am a gentleman and a catholic. And now to return to your daughter: I love her beyond any woman I ever beheld—and if you will deign to bestow her on me, I am willing to take her without any other dower than her lovely self—to me more welcome than the treasures of Mexico, or Peru."

"Justice demands the truth," replied the duke, relaxing from his accustomed austerity. "I must tell you, it was my eldest daughter who cautioned me against you, and she must declare her author: which done, Angela (for I can doubt no longer) is your's."

Lord Liffey, in pity to Elvira, begged that the business might be canvassed no further. But to this the duke returned a positive negative, and insisted that his lordship, with the corrigidor, should accompany him home—for the purpose of having the matter elucidated.

Elvira soon found, that her assertion to the prejudice of Liffey was unfounded and, with blushes, confessed she was indebted to Don Rodorigo for the account—who had represented the Hibernian as a needy adventurer, who sought to ennoble his own plebeian blood, by allying himself to the duke. She acknowledged she had a sinister view to answer, in propagating the report, for which she humbly entreated pardon;—and declared that her future days should be devoted to penance, in the sanctuary to which she had been the instrument of accelerating her sister's departure.

The duke, as a proof of his confidence in Liffey, now gave him a letter for the abbess, instructing her to deliver the person of Angela to the bearer. As he was about to depart, his faithful servant (who had been in search of him the whole night) burst into the room, and threw himself on his knees before his master, crying:—

"*Arrah!* why would you leave poor Murdoch behind you, and have all the fighting to yourself? When I saw you jump from the wall, and heard the swords going, I ran around to the gate of the nunnery, in a crack—and there, who should I meet, but one of the duke's servants! Where's my master, you big blockhead? says I.—'Where you'll never see him again,' says he.—Are you sure of that? says I—and without the *laist* ceremony, gave him a *Dungarvon hoist*, and laid him *clain* in the mud—there, says I, stick that in your pipe, and smoke it! and as soon as you get home, don't forget to step up the kitchen-chimeny, with a *clain* shirt under your arm—for you want one. I did not stop to see whether he got up again—but set off like a cat after her kitten; and hearing that they had brought you here, I came to try if I could save your life, by dying with you!"

His lordship assured him, all his perils were at an end: that he was reconciled to the duke, and was going to fetch the daughter of that nobleman from the monastery—and ordered Murdoch to remain where he was, till his return.

"No, no," replied Murdoch, "if you are for that place again, devil burn me! But Mr. Mc. Cludderough will go with you!"

So he did, in defiance of his master's order—and as they went, Murdoch thus addressed him:

"I have a small bit of a favour to ask of you, my lord. As you are going to be married to Donna Angela, I hope you will let me enter into the holy state myself, with Mrs. Flora —like master, like man. The *crature* is as fond as a tame kitten, (but she can't help that) and says, she will go with me to my little potato estate in Ireland. Lazarillo offered me half the shoes in his shop (by way of paying her fortune in ready money) but if he would have given me all, I would not have taken any, *becase* that would have been putting him to an unnecessary expence for nothing—seeing she would have no use for 'em among the *bog-trotters*. And so your honour, *will* I be married?"

Liffey gave his ready assent—and being now at the gate of the convent, delivered his letter, and received his beloved Angela from the lady abbess. Their meeting may be better conceived than depicted. She told him, that having made a confidant of the nun he had seen her with in the garden, she had betrayed her trust, and the emissaries of her father were consequently stationed to intercept her flight.

The duke received her with more tenderness than he had ever evinced towards her, and the morning that united her to her lover, saw the repentant Elvira enter the convent of Saint Mary—never to return. Liffey carried his beloved wife to Ireland (attended by the faithful Murdoch and his spouse) and the remainder of his years, (for he bade adieu to *the tented field!*)—glided away, in peace and happiness.

CHAP. V.

Upon his bloody finger he doth wear
A precious ring———

TITUS ANDRONICUS.[1]

Beauty provoketh thieves sooner than gold.

AS YOU LIKE IT.[2]

THE current bore the unfortunate Aurora into a deep cavern. When suspended animation returned, she looked around in dismay for the means of escaping—but found it impossible to return—as the water penetrated many yards into the cavity. At a distance, in an opposite direction, she descried a light—and tottering through a long passage, that branched out into various others, she entered a spacious vaulted apartment, formed of solid rock.—Against the sides were suspended swords, shields, cuirasses, helmets, and other implements of war; and in the centre,

1 Shakespeare, *Titus Andronicus* (1594), 2.3.226-227.
2 1.3.104.

stood a large table, plentifully stored with cold viands and flaggons of wine—of the last, Aurora, who was nigh fainting, tasted, and found her spirits recruited by it.

All seemed mysterious—she neither heard or saw a living creature—the inscription on the tablet, relative to the murder, and to the banditti, who infested the mountains, recurred to her and she conjectured this to be one of their secret haunts. She took a flambeau, and lighted it by a lamp, that was suspended from the roof, and ascended a flight of steps, at the opposite extremity of the cavern to that by which she entered. At the summit, a massy iron door impeded her passage—and she descended in an agony of despair.

On each side of the cavern were small cabins, and in one part a door much larger than the rest, and rudely formed: which she opened—but the putrid stench which she inhaled caused her to shudder. Nevertheless, as it might be the road to her emancipation, she proceeded, and after passing through a long passage, found herself in a cemetery.—Several bodies in their living apparel, were lying about, one of which quickly caught her attention. It was in a green velvet doublet, flashed with rose colour—the very same she had seen Carlos wear. And to leave no doubt that it was his corpse, on his dead finger was the identical ring she had given him, when he rescued her from the ravishers at Toledo. The discovery was too much for her, and she fainted.

When she again opened her eyes, she beheld a stranger, busily employed in attempting to revive her—and the bosom of her pilgrim's dress being thrown open, she surmised, and truly, that her sex was discovered.

The savage air of the stranger struck terror into her. He was an athletic figure, in a scarlet doublet and trunks, and a breast-plate and helmet. His shaggy brows partly concealed his large eye-balls, with which he glared on the prostrate maid—and which, added to his curved nose, and black bushy beard, gave him an appearance bordering on ferocity.

"How come you here, my dainty damsel?" demanded he, in a hoarse voice. "By the mass! my angel, you must have had dealings with the devil, to find your way into this place!"

Aurora told him candidly of her disaster, in falling from the bridge, and of her being carried by the waves into the mouth of the cavern and solicited permission to depart.

"Ha! ha! ha!" cried he—"let you depart!—Can you see *fool* written on the forehead of Ramirez?—No, no—I cannot suffer you to go: you are a delicate morsel, and worthy to become my wife.—Mind, I mean in name—as to the idle ceremony of marriage, that we must dispense with. I am at the head of fifty as brave fellows as ever used at Toledo to cry, 'Stand!' Attend me then, and I'll shew you to them as their mistress."

She implored him, by every argument in her power to release her, or to deprive her of existence, rather than persist in his diabolical intent. But to this he was as deaf as the wind, and had laid his unhallowed hands upon her sacred person, when they were joined by another man—a perfect contrast to the first. His person was tall and grace-ful—his face manly and interesting, with a full dark eye, and an aquiline nose. He wore a yellow doublet, the trunks and sleeves of which were flashed with green: a polished breast-plate glittered on his chest, and his fair countenance was shaded with a profusion of black feathers which fell from a large russet-coloured hat.

"Your companions tarry for you, Ramirez," said he. "But, who is this stranger?"

"A fair lady, whom I intend to honour with my

embraces," replied Ramirez. "Inform my comrades, I will attend them instantly."

"Oh! do not leave me!" exclaimed Aurora. "*Your* countenance bespeaks a soul of sensibility. Haply there is some one in the world, dear to your recollection: then fancy you see them bending beneath the power of insult, without the ability to resent—and save me from this ruffian!"

"Lady," replied the man, "I need no further incitement to defend a helpless woman, than what the impulse of nature dictates. How chances it I find you here?"

"What is that to thee?" demanded Ramirez. "Go, and say I will join the band presently. What! do you hesitate to obey my mandate?"

"I do," said the other. "You are my captain, and I am bound to shew obedience: but when humanity gives the word of command, all other ties of duty sink before her imperious voice."

"Begone, or dread my vengeance!" cried Ramirez, fire flashing from his eyes.

"I despise it," replied Ricardo (so was the other called) "and will release this fair one from your power, at the hazard of my life."

They grew still higher in dispute—fire flashed from their eyes, and they unsheathed their falchions. They struck with uncommon violence, and sparks issued from each stroke. At length, Ricardo elevating his well-tempered blade, discharged it with such resistless force, against the head of his antagonist, that he dropt, lifeless, on the ground, and his groan bellowed through the rock.

At the same instant, the banditti made their appearance, and seeing their leader lifeless, and Ricardo standing over the body, with his sword drawn, and bloody, were about to wreak their vengeance on him, when he, with great presence of mind, related what had passed, and told them if he had deprived them of their captain, he was ready to offer them another, in himself, and concluded by demanding if there was one among them who would scruple to spill his heart's blood in the service of a woman.

"None! none!" exclaimed the band, almost unanimously. "Long live our new captain, the brave Ricardo!"

"I thank you," replied he, "and shall study to merit a continuance of your good opinion."

He then took the hand of Aurora, and led her to the great cavern, whither they were followed by the banditti. He seated her on his right hand, and pressed her to partake of the refreshments with such a cordial, but respectful air, that he imperceptibly won her good opinion. His manner was unlike the rest of the company—for while they pushed the goblet around with glee, and laughed at the tale rehearsed, low, but deep groans heaved his manly chest, and Aurora imagined she saw a tear more than once glisten in his eye.

Their repast ended, he led her to one of the cabins, where she was to sleep—and ere he left her, she anxiously demanded whose corpse it was she had seen in the cemetery of the cavern, as before described.

"I know not," quoth Ricardo. "'Tis now some months since he first joined us. He said he was flying from the pursuit of justice (having assassinated one who had grossly insulted him) but ever refused to divulge his name. He used to talk much too of a lady, whom he dearly loved," (and here Ricardo sighed) "and whom circumstances had obliged him to desert. I always thought him of high birth, for his demeanour on first joining us, was most gentlemanly—but he soon lost himself, gave way to inebriety, and finally lost his life in a drunken quarrel with another of the band.—But it is late—a good repose, and angels watch over and guard you!"

So saying, he departed, with melancholy depicted in his face, leaving Aurora a prey to misery. She sat some time meditating on the unhappy end of the still regretted Carlos—when finding herself unable to sleep, she left her chamber, ascended the steps, and the iron door being now open, sallied out to enjoy the coolness of the night-breeze.

CHAP. VI.

Fear not, he bears an honourable mind,
And will not use a woman lawlessly.
THE TWO GENTLEMEN OF VERONA.[1]

ON the summit of a rock, whose base was washed by the roaring stream—Aurora beheld Ricardo leaning upon his sword, and gazing on the moon—while the night breeze fanned the drops which stood upon his clay-cold temple, and heavy groans burst from his manly breast.

At length, he gave vent to his thoughts in soliloquy, and poured forth the feelings of his surcharged heart in the following words:—

"Yes," said he, "it must be done! A good long night to all! No blushing morn will dawn again, for me—my sun of life is set for ever! I have outlived the respect of every virtuous person—and which is worse, my own esteem—and now possess the good opinion of a set of wretches, only, who honour me for my vices: and as though my measure were not full, before, this heart (which I thought dead to all the softer passions) is now become the slave of hopeless love.—Baneful reflection! this is thy antidote!" (and he drew a dagger) "this instrument, o'er which time and eternity embrace!—Terrible key! that opest the door of ever-

---

1 Shakespeare, *The Two Gentlemen of Verona* (1598), 5.3.13-14.

lasting freedom, tell me, whither wilt thou lead me?—I shrink at the very thought! But wherefore shrink!—The boundless idea of eternity confounds me. What, am I become a coward? Is death, which oft I have encountered in his ghastliest forms, become a terror to me?—No—this must prove I have courage to shake off this mortal coil!"

He raised the dagger to perpetrate his fell intent, when his arm was arrested—and turning to reprimand the officious meddler, he beheld Aurora.

"Sweet intruder!" cried he, "in whose fair visage charity is personified, wherefore this cruelty?"

"Cruelty?" repeated Aurora in amazement.

"Aye, refined cruelty," quoth he.—"When I had freighted my bark with resolution, and was about to launch into an unknown sea, thou hast prevented me—and I have again to encounter the horrors of anticipation with which my busy fancy furnishes me.—I prithee, leave me!"

"I cannot: pardon me if I say I will not, in your present state of mind. You had great care for me, when threatened by the menaces of the ruffian Ramirez, you interposed in my behalf, and rescued me from worse than death. Let me now have some care for you."

"Think not of it—you owe me nothing.—Man is, or ought to be, the natural protector of the other sex; and when he degrades himself by offering violence where he should defend, raise the arm of a dwarf against a giant's strength, and the all-wise justice of Providence will befriend the weak."

"Wonderful!" exclaimed Aurora, involuntarily—"can it be, that a mind possessing such a sentiment can associate with wretches?—With—"

"With robbers," said Ricardo—"never hesitate. But judge not too severely of me. I am no voluntary thief: circumstances (the effect of dissipation) have driven me to this disgraceful calling. I am an outcast from society, bearing about with me (like the first murderer) the sin of disobedience, and the anathema of a beloved——I cannot think of it! it tortures me!"

"But is it too late to retrieve your errors?" inquired Aurora, in a voice which soothed the impetuosity of the robber. "Surely no—you may yet return to virtue—more welcome to the Almighty's eye, than twenty who have never trespassed."

"To virtue! to virtue!" repeated Ricardo. "Behold yon planet," (pointing to the moon) "holds her nocturnal course through azure skies, unclouded. Why is my heart choaked with the black vapours of despair?—The trees and shrubs put forth their buds, and enjoy the genial breath of spring. Why do I alone inhale the blast of hell? The spirit of peace pervades all—the whole world is as a family with one father.—But, alas! not a father to me!—I alone, am singled out from the circle of the righteous and rivetted to vice with chains of adamant!"

He gnashed his teeth, in agony, and smote his forehead vehemently. After a pause, and in a voice that shewed the paroxysm was then subsiding, he continued:

"Would I had been born a beggar! I would slave till the blood should trickle upon my temples, to purchase the pleasure of a few hours sleep—the exquisite delight of a single tear!——There was a time when they flowed freely from me. Days, never—never to return!—Mourn, oh nature, with me!—they are irrecoverably gone!"

Aurora's heart bled for him, and she regarded him as a superior being. She spoke to him in the most soothing accents religion could furnish her withal—and implored him for her sake, to calm his transports.

"For your sake?" replied he. "What is it I would not do, when thus adjured? Yes, I will endeavour to be calm—your arguments are irresistible. 'Though you were the innocent cause of my attempting to rush, with all my sins upon my head, into the presence of my Creator. But you must leave this place, I will to-morrow conduct you to a spot of safety: and when in happier times blest with some honourable partner, you think of past events, do not dispute the memory of the unhappy Ricardo—*who loved you!*"

Aurora shrunk from him.

"Fear not, amiable creature!" resumed he—"too well I know the distance fate has placed between us, to wish to link such virtue to my vice. To-morrow we part for ever! Had it been otherwise, I would have buried my secret deep in my heart, though it had devoured it, 'ere I would have disclosed it to you. 'Tis told—and I will ne'er insult your ear with a repetition of my folly. Now let me beseech you to retire, you must be sadly worn with terror and fatigue. Allow me to reconduct you to the cavern and early in the morning I will awake you for your journey."

"I fear to leave you," said Aurora.—"Tell me, and truly, have you banished all thoughts of the fatal purpose, which I (by heaven's dispensation) prevented?"

"On my honour! I—honour!" repeated he with an indignant smile.——"Yes—let me repeat it—and though a robber, believe me, my honour given, was never violated!"—"There," continued he, dashing his dagger into the waves beneath, "there I discard the fatal instrument—and with it my fell purpose. Thy words, like the resistless voice of angels, have changed my unhallowed purpose and made my heart o'erflow with penitence."

He led her down the steps—and in the large cavern lay many of the banditti, buried in sleep, from the effect of their late libations. Aurora shrunk as she reflected on the contiguity of the situation in which she was to spend the remainder of the night. Ricardo saw her disgust—and rightfully surmising the occasion, bade her fear nothing, but rest in perfect security—for that he would answer she should not be molested—wished her a sound repose, and she entered the cell. There, musing on the occurrences of the night, and marvelling how one, possessed of the graceful, courtly manners, and exalted mind of Ricardo, should have been driven to his present wretched occupation—and imploring heaven's forgiveness, that she had been innocently, the cause of Ramirez's untimely death, she sunk into a sweet sleep; from which she did not awake 'till the voice of Ricardo told her the sun was risen and that it was time to depart.

At the door of her vaulted chamber, she was met by Ricardo—who led her to a table spread with various sorts of fruit and goats' milk. While she partook thereof, she regretted to see the countenance of her deliverer pale, his eyes blood-shot, and his hair dishevelled—and inquired anxiously if he was indisposed.

He evaded answering the question, and pressed her departure. At the summit of the steps, the iron door impeded their passage, which the manly strength of Ricardo wrenched open—and when he closed it after them, our wanderer could perceive no trace of it—so artfully was it concealed by moss and briars.

They set out on their journey—and about noon, came to a small comfortable house, encircled with fig-trees.

"Here," said Ricardo, "our journey ends. In that hospitable mansion you will be safe. But, as I may not have another opportunity to address you, allow me to give you a few words of caution ere we part. What chance may have driven you to your present state, I know not—nor does it become me to inquire. I wish only, that you should not satisfy the interrogatories of any one—who, you are not well convinced is your sincere friend. For trust me, there are many who dive into the misfortunes of their fellow-creatures to satiate an idle curiosity or for the purpose of betraying the unwary and inexperienced. I know the world, and have had damning proofs of its insincerity. But Saints will look, and watch over innocence like your's —and to their protection will Ricardo (if his prayers avail) commend you."

Aurora returned him unfeigned thanks, and they proceeded to the house. At the gate they were met by three fine children (the eldest about ten, the youngest five years old) who ran with out-stretched arms to welcome Aurora's companion, exclaiming:—

"Oh! father, father, here's Don Ricardo!"—Two of them took each a hand of his—the third running before and crying—"Don Ricardo is come!"

At the threshold stood an old man, who bade the robber welcome, in the most cordial manner. Ricardo returned his civilities, and introduced Aurora to him as a lady who was flying from persecution, and had been obliged to assume the habit of a pilgrim, to elude her pursuers. He further said, he was much interested in her fortunes, and that the old man would oblige him by introducing her to the superior of the neighbouring monastery.

This he promised to do, with an assurance that he felt himself imminently happy in having an opportunity to make a small return of the kindness shewn him by Ricardo.

The robber interrupted him abruptly, and begged him to be silent on the subject. The table was now spread with some good but homely food; and at the conclusion of their meal, he arose, shook his host's hand, and carried that of Aurora to his lips, ejaculated a blessing on her—and with an internal struggle, burst from the house.

"An excellent man!" observed the old host—"this world can boast of very few like him. In his first visit here, it seemed as if my guardian-angel had come to snatch me from the jaws of desperation."

This encomium on her preserver raised him still higher in Aurora's esteem; for it seemed not the utterance of adulation, but an involuntary burst of gratitude—and was hailed by her as the meed of his worth.

It was settled, that our heroine should remain at her present abode that night; and on the following day her host was to accompany her to the convent of Saint Clare— whose glittering vanes were visible from the place where she sat. She determined to take the veil, but in vain did fancy anticipate the contentment of a cloister: she thought of Carlos with many a bitter pang; and instead of restoring to the hallowed walls, a voluntary recluse from the enchantments of the world, she, (like the suicide) rushed from its disappointments—unconscious whither.

It was in the evening (after the children were retired) that a repetition of sighs on the part of Aurora occasioned her companion to address her, with a wish, that she would combat her melancholy, and recollect that Providence, however she might feel the wound, inflicted it for her own good, and would, in his own time, pour balm into her hurt.

"Oh! my good father," said she, "you know not what I suffer. My friends deceased; and one, into whose custody I had resigned my virgin-heart, has fled, unworthy of the love he took pains to obtain. Alas! what have I to hope?"

"Every thing," replied the old man; "for I am sure no guilty pang invades your breast.—Oh! God! what are the sharpest sufferings, compared to those of an accusing conscience? To shun retrospection as too hideous for the brain, nor dare look forward to futurity; but in thought, forsaken by God and man, wish that existence may terminate in this world for ever! You marvel at my words: but know, you behold a wretch stained with a crime at which humanity shudders—and the tortures I have described, I speak from self-experience.——But," continued he, in a calmer tone, and raising his eyes to heaven, "though happiness can ne'er be mine again, I have, by prayer and fasting, addressed him, who never shuts the ear to supplication—and I wait with patience till my weary soul shall be released. You look doubtingly—but do not think worse of me than I deserve. If an old man's tale will not be tedious to you, you shall hear mine: and though you will find little to entertain, it is a caution to the impetuous, and as I shall have occasion to speak of the virtues of Don Ricardo, that may compensate for the rest—for he is the bravest, the most generous of men."

Aurora made answer, that she should consider herself obliged by the recital, if he thought it would not open the wounds of his heart and make them bleed afresh. The old man replied, that was impossible, for they had never been healed—and thus began.

CHAP. VII.

> The ways of heav'n are dark and intricate,
> Puzzled in mazes, and perplex'd with errors—
> Our understanding traces them in vain,
> Lost and bewilder'd in the fruitless search—
> Nor sees with how much art the windings run,
> Nor where the regular confusion ends.

ADDISON.[1]

"Don Lopez was esteemed one of the wealthiest merchants in Saragossa; but severe and unlooked-for losses suddenly reduced him, and he fled from his merciless creditors, to avoid the horrors of the galleys. He left behind

1 Joseph Addison (1672-1719), *Cato: A Tragedy* (1712), 1.1.47-53.

him a disconsolate wife, and a daughter sixteen years of age, whom he consigned to the care of a sincere friend, named Pedro, and who was the only one that did not, swallow-like, forsake him, in the winter of adversity.

"At Don Pedro's house, it was my lot to see his young charge, Viola;—whose sweet simplicity of manners captivated me at our first interview. I attached myself to her, during my whole visit, and had reason to flatter myself my assiduities were not displeasing to her—or to her mother, who also was of the party.

"I returned home with my own mother, who evinced no common portion of disapprobation against me, for my civilities to the strangers; asking, if I knew on whom I had been lavishing my time and attention?—I frankly told her I did not, but that I should make it my business to ascertain that point immediately; as the younger lady had made so complete a conquest of my heart that I meant to ask her hand in marriage.

'Foolish boy!' cried my mother, whose pride was her only failing, 'I'll cure you of these love-sick notions.—Know, Isidor, this girl, whose artful blandishments have tricked you of your affections, is the daughter of a bankrupt merchant—a fugitive from his native country—a fellow, in whose veins not a drop of noble blood flows, and who, I dare say, cannot trace his ancestry three generations upwards.—These beggarly relatives are supported by the mistaken bounty of Don Pedro, who disgraces his noble descent by the acquaintance, and through his connections, the crafty mother I suppose, reckons to match her low-born daughter with nobility.—Now, sir, what say you?'

"That my passion is increased by your intelligence, said I: that so pure is my affection, I exult in the idea of her inferiority of birth, as it will enable me to shew the disinterestedness of my love, and to elevate her to a sphere, which will call the blush of comparative shame into the cheeks of many of her sex, who have naught to recommend them, but their high descent. Unfeeling prejudice! which I despise.—I may give rank to her; but in so doing, I shall receive, not bestow, dignity.

'Santa Maria!' cried my mother, 'can this be a descendant of the noble house of Guzman? grovelling idiot!—where is the lofty spirit of your forefathers?—But it cannot be that you are in earnest.'

"Having affirmed my intention of offering to espouse Donna Viola, with an oath, my mother rejoined:—

"'Tis well, Sir, that I am acquainted with your want of pride: for know, that I will not give or leave a single pistole to you, if you persist in your weak intention. How you may relish love in a cottage, time may prove—but affection will rarely stand the test of poverty.'

"I felt myself nettled, and replied, my aunt's liberality would secure me from the trial; or should I be exposed to it, that I had too much of the pride of the Guzmans, to sue to her for relief.

"So I ended my conversation.

"I immediately waited on Don Pedro; and requesting him to be explicit, asked if Viola had any favoured admirer.—He told me, so far from having a favoured lover, he was convinced she had never been addressed on that subject. I was charmed with this communication and freely imparted my intention to him; in which he generously offered me his assistance, and I had the supreme delight of being received as the destined husband of my Viola.

"The day was fixed for our nuptials, and many friends invited to participate in our happiness, when my Viola's mother was taken off, by a fit of apoplexy, and all our joy converted into mourning. I watched my beloved during the paroxysms of her grief; and at length had the delight to see it somewhat lulled, and the delay of my bliss seemed to be amply recompensed.

"And now I come to that period of my tale, which robbed me of peace, and rendered me one of the most miserable and guilty of men.

"I had an officious servant (as such will always be about the wealthy) who desired to speak with me, on a business that concerned my nearest and my dearest interests. He told me that a good understanding subsisted between himself and Donna Viola's woman: that she kept nothing a secret from him, and had in confidence, acquainted him, that a strange cavalier had been introduced to her lady in her chamber the night before.

"I was not of a very jealous temper, and a something flashed across my mind that my mother (for I knew she would descend to any measures where family-pride was at stake) had bribed him to calumniate my mistress, in hope of breaking off the match.

"Under that impression, I seized the fellow roughly, and should have emolated him to my resentment—but the trembling wretch fell on his knees, and besought me to calm my choler; and if he did not satisfy me as to the truth of what he had advanced, he would willingly lay down his life as the forfeit. I released him, and he took a letter from his pocket, saying, it had been delivered to him by Viola's woman, as a proof of her veracity, and that she had received it from the gallant in question, to give to her mistress.

"I have preserved," continued Isidor; "and will read it to you."

He arose and went to his cabinet—whence he took a paper, and read thus:

'In our last short interview, I had not time to say all I

wished. But my beloved Viola may expect me this night, as the clock strikes twelve; when I shall hope to pass a few hours in the enviable society of her, who is now, my only solace.—Till twelve, farewell!'

"I was wound up to a pitch of madness," said Don Isidor, "at the perusal of this fatal letter. Grief, rage, and wounded pride assailed me, by turns, and made my mind a hell.—One minute, I meditated going to Viola, upbraiding her with her perfidy, and tearing myself from her forever. The next, I resolved to call my rival to the field, but this design was frustrated by the foul dæmon of revenge—who whispered it would be but a poor satisfaction, to stake my own existence on the issue—and the result of these cogitations, was the dreadful resolve of assassination.

"My servant gave the waiting-woman the letter again, and bribed her to conceal me, where I was to witness the assignation. Between the hours of eleven and twelve, I and my servant (for he would accompany me) went to the house of Don Pedro, and were conducted into a closet, that commanded a view of my mistress's dressing room. Thence, I beheld her reading a letter; which I supposed to be the one I had intercepted, for she kissed it repeatedly. I was almost tempted to rush out and sacrifice her to my resentment—but I restrained my transports, to make my vengeance more complete.

"I had not tarried long, when a cavalier, muffled in a long cloak entered, and caught the lady to his breast—straining her close in his embrace, and saying:

'To die in her arms was all he wished.'

"I could refrain no longer, being wound up to ungovernable fury—but rushed from my ambush, and exclaiming:

"'Wretch accursed! be thy wish gratified!' ran my sword up to the hilt, into his body. He staggered, and faintly articulating:

'*I die my daughter!*'

"Oh! God!" returned Isidor, his eyes rolling, and large drops of anguish standing on his clammy forehead, "what were my sensations, at the utterance of those words! I wished the earth to gape, and bury me and my crimes, in its centre!—Oh! let no one give a licence to their passions, whose influence, like the moon's, tramples on reason and oft converts a life of happiness, into one of heart-gnawing anguish and remorse! By their fell power was I robbed of peace and innocence, and doomed to misery and despair!"

He paused for a few minutes, overcome by the intenseness of his feelings—and then resumed.

"When I beheld my Viola, insensible on the dead body of her father, and contemplated the whole as the work of my own dire hand, I should have fallen on my sword, had I not been prevented by my servant. He strove to reason with me and intimated the necessity of my immediate flight, ere I was intercepted. I suffered myself to be led away by him, more anxious to avoid the reproachful eyes of the orphan I had made, than to preserve my own existence.—He conducted me to a small pavilion, at the end of my mother's garden, whither he brought two of my fleetest horses, saying, he was ready to accompany me in my flight.

"I mounted one of the steeds, but peremptorily forbade his attendance—for I could not but consider him as the cause of my guilt, and the sight of him disgusted me. I rode from the city—and giving my horse the rein, I pursued my way the whole night, and at daybreak, finding myself near the opening of a wood, I entered it, tied my steed to the stump of a tree, and remained[1] there till evening. I then resumed my solitary journey—and the next morning brought me to this house—when worn with

---

1 In the first edition, 'tyed' and 'remaining'.

corporeal and mental sufferings, I could proceed no further. It was tenanted by an aged woman and her niece—
and they attended me with unremitting diligence, during
my illness.

"I had been here a month, and was recovering my
strength apace, when I was alarmed by the screams of the
young woman—and hastened to the room, where I found
her lamenting over her aunt, who lay speechless on the
bed, having been struck with the palsy.

"It was many days ere she was able to articulate—when
sitting between me and her niece, the latter congratulated
her on being better, and with the sanguine hope of youth,
said, she hoped to see her perfectly restored, and that very
soon.

"The old woman shook her head, and replied:—
'It is in vain to flatter myself, or you—I am going to
another, and a much better world. Nay, do not weep my
child! it is for your sake alone, that I leave this transitory
vale, with the least pang of regret. When I am gone, what
pitying heart will soothe my Inis! bitter anguish!—What
friendly hand will wipe her tears away, and be a protector
to her?—None! None!'

"Not so, by Saint Antony! cried I. I will soothe and protect her: and never, never, will I desert her.

"The old woman pressed my hand, and rejoined:
'I thank you! 'tis christian-like to smooth the pillow
of death, and I thank you————But,' and she paused,
'circumstances may occur to deprive her of your care—
engagements, which you are not aware of, may interfere.
I must be explicit. I cannot die in peace, except I leave her
a legal protector. I have five hundred crowns, which, with
this house are your's, if you will take her for your wife. I
see you are startled at my proposal, and that it is unaccept-
able. Well, then, I am doomed to leave my child destitute.'

"Tears rolled down her cheek, and they went to my very heart. I saw a fellow-creature unhappy, in her dying hours, who had befriended me, and I had the power to alleviate her grief.—My own felicity was destroyed—I had nothing left to hope or fear in this world—and gratitude bade me bestow comfort on my hostess—at the same time that, I thought, it would, in some measure, expiate my heinous guilt.

"Impressed with this idea, I was willing, provided there was no repugnance in the other party, to take her niece's hand. The blush upon her cheek answered, I was not indifferent to her; while the joy which illumined the dying eyes of her relative, repaid me amply for my acquiescence.

"Her confessor called that evening, and united me to Inis, in the presence of her aunt—who took our hands, as soon as the ceremony was over, pressed them to her heart, and casting a look of gratitude to heaven, fell back on the bosom of her niece, and expired—as though life had lingered, to see her wish accomplished—and then departed!

"I shall pass over the grief of my bride, and inform you, that during ten years, we were without children: at the termination of that period, Inis gave to my arms a daughter—and since then, three sons—whose innocent prattle has beguiled many hours, that would otherwise have been spent in painful retrospection. Three winters ago, I lost my wife—and the education of her offspring has been my chief employment since.

"And now I come to the circumstance, which will give me occasion to speak of the excellent qualities of that good man—Don Ricardo.

"A young nobleman, who inhabits a castle in this neighbourhood, felt, or pretended a passion for my daughter.—He professed the most ardent regard—but regretted that he could not marry her immediately, as his father was of an inexorable temper, his whole dependence was on him, and he would never forgive his son's marrying one so much inferior to him in point of rank.

"Insolent libeller, he little thought the blood which flowed in her veins, was superior to his own!

"Under this embarrassment, he requested her to dispense with the idle ceremony for the present, and to consider him as her husband in every respect—vowing the priest should join their hands so soon as his father (who was very old) should be no more.

"What shall I say?—Young and inexperienced, struck with his fine person, and flattered by his addresses, she yielded her honour a prey to his illicit desires.

"A deep melancholy pervaded her manner—of which, I strove to ascertain the source, but in vain—till at length, her shame discovered *itself,* and I had little trouble to learn the author of her ruin.

"At his next visit, I taxed him with having robbed her of her dearest possession, virtue—and insisted on his doing her justice. To this, with vast indifference, he replied, if a thousand pistoles would compound the felony he had committed, and pay the price of the pillage, he was ready to make amends—but no further. I was irritated, to be used with such contempt—but the winter of age was strewed upon my head, and I was unable to cope with youth. I was therefore obliged to content myself with forbidding him the house—which order he treated with the same scorn that he had done my expostulation.

"Things were in this situation, when a person knocked at my humble portal and craved admittance at a very late hour. I opened the door—and saw a cavalier, pale and bleeding, leaning upon his sword. My daughter and I brought him in and staunched his wound—which, though deep, was not of a serious nature.

"That cavalier was Don Ricardo—who, observing my daughter's dejection, joked her on the occasion, and imputed the cause to love. The fond girl burst into tears, and retired: when I, struck by the open countenance and ingenuous manners of my guest, divulged her story.

"Next day, her seducer visited her; and Don Ricardo thus addressed him:

'You are, I understand, affianced to this damsel—and after having enjoyed the rights of a husband, under the sanction of a marriage-promise, you basely shrink from the fulfillment of your word. If you think proper to espouse her, whom under a specious mask, you have deeply injured, I will give her a dower your pride need not blush to take. If not, behold in me her champion—and one determined to see justice done to her. We are here, man to man, nor can your boasted lineage, or aught else, save valour, avail you in the contest. Speak, how do you resolve?'

"He embraced her as his wife, in preference to measuring swords with the brave stranger—but, from that time, we have never seen him—and his desertion sent my poor girl to an untimely grave.

"We have often been honoured with the visits of the generous Don Ricardo, in whom all the virtues seem combined; and heaven will, I trust, shower those blessings ten-fold, on his head, which it is his study to dispense to his fellow-creatures. Further than his name I have never been able to ascertain—but that he is of noble extraction his dignified mien fully declares—however that be, his virtues exalt him in my opinion, far beyond what I could feel from birth and fortune.

CHAP. VIII.

I've heard, but not believ'd, the spirits of the dead
May walk again—

THE WINTER'S TALE.[1]

AURORA bade adieu to the sheltering roof of Isidor, who introduced her to the abbess of the convent, and she was received with much kindness by her.—Nay, so much did the holy mother gain on her confidence, that she related her history without reserve. St. Bridget, that was her name, listened to her with attention, comforted her with many religious precepts, and exhorted her to dedicate her future days to the service of her maker—nor again trust to the temptations of this world.

Her fair auditor promised implicit obedience to her admonitions; and could she have effaced the memory of the guilty Carlos from her heart she might have been content.

As this fatal recollection preyed upon her spirits, it deprived her of rest; and it was her frequent custom to rise, in the dead of night, when all was still within the walls, and by the light of the tapers, which burnt on the altar, to tell her beads.

One night (as she rose from her devotions) suddenly a tall figure wrapt in white, burst from behind a monument at a few paces distant. She fell upon her knees, and crossing her bosom, recommended herself to the protection of the Virgin. The figure glided towards her, threw back his mantle, and pointed to a scar on his breast; with a fearful

1 3.3.15-16.

eye, Aurora glanced at his features, and beheld the pallid countenance of the robber—Ramirez!

The figure remained for a few seconds, in a menacing posture, gazing on her; and then, as suddenly vanished—leaving her wrapt in terror and amazement.

"I have offended my God!" said she—"the blood of a fellow-creature is on my head, and the murdered is allowed to leave his grave, to reproach me!—Oh! father of mercy! how shall I avert thy Almighty wrath?"

The idea of having seen the spirit of Ramirez haunted her, day and night, and imbittered her hours. She wished to persuade herself, that she had been deceived by fancy, aided by the awful horror of the night: but the angry glare with which the figure had gazed on her, and the wound to which he had pointed, were too powerfully impressed on her memory to be the produce of illusion.

A month had elapsed from the appearance of this mystic visitant (during which period Aurora had ceased her nightly orisons at the altar) when the abbess asked her company in the garden one night. While they were taking their walk, two men darted from behind a hedge, and seized our heroine—while the superior fled towards the building, crying for help.

The men wrapt a veil close round Aurora's head, so as to muffle her eyes and mouth, and conducted her through a small door in the wall, then placed her on a horse, one of the ruffians mounting behind her, and set off at a round gallop.

They rode for five or six hours, when by the clattering of the horse's hoofs, she conjectured they were crossing a drawbridge. She was then dismounted, and led up a long flight of stairs; when the bandage was removed from her eyes, and the ruffians, having set down a lamp, left the room and locked the door.

She was in a small chamber, without a window, and whose bare walls struck a melancholy chill upon her. She was undisturbed for a time, and passed the interval in prayers and lamentations, when, raising her eyes towards heaven, in mental ejaculation, they rested on the dreaded figure of Ramirez!—His expression was more ferocious than on the former occasion: he menaced her so maliciously, that she put her hands before her eyes, to shut out his hated form—and on again looking up, he was gone.

As she was marvelling on this second mystery, the door of her dungeon was opened, and a no-less dreaded object stood before her—in the person of Rodorigo: his face was suffused with the flush of intemperance, and the wild stare of his blood-shot eyes declared he had been drinking freely.

"Still in tears?" cried he, with an insulting look.—"Thy source of sorrow is inexhaustible. But let that rest. I come to welcome you once more to the Castle of Henares; 'though, to speak sooth, your abrupt departure (without one kind farewel) hardly demands such courtesy. I came to say——"

"Then I must hear you," interrupted Aurora, indignantly, "for Rodorigo de Henares is become a noble lord!"

"That is the subject I am about to address you on. Antonio sleeps in the grave of his ancestors, and I am paramount. You know the love of the old count for you, which survived even death. The affection of the father you must repay to the son. Nay, start not! though, indeed, the thought must be highly flattering—that Rodorigo spurns beneath his feet the proffers of our noblest dames, and comes to offer to an helpless orphan, his hand and rich domains."

"Were I more helpless than I am (but that is hardly possible) rather would I perish, than accept thy vaunted offer."

"Not so violent. True, I cannot stoop to sue to you, like a love-sick Corydon—who sighs out his amorous moans to caves and fountains. Rodorigo entreats; and if rejected, he commands."

"Command!—Poor worm!—what if thy command be answered with contempt?"

"That I heed not," rejoined he: "I marry you for the wealth my doting father left you—no other motive induces me. And for that reason did I suborn the abbess to deliver, Ramirez to bring, you to me.—Foolish girl!—I received a letter from her, as soon as she knew your story; and with Ramirez (who had traced you to your sanctuary) she was my tool. Now mark me. Dare to persist in your refusal, I will drag you by the hair to the chapel; and with a dagger to your throat, will I extort the nuptial oath. Aye, gnash your teeth, and let fire sparkle in your eyes: your rage delights me—it makes you ten times more desirable.—Come to the altar! my people are waiting there to congratulate their lady—and this moment I will force you thither."

He seized her rudely, and in spite of her struggles, dragged her to the well-known chapel of Henares castle, which was illuminated, and filled with the household, each of whom secretly pitied the unhappy victim.

"Father! proceed!" cried Rodorigo, forcing her to the altar.

The aged chaplain (who obeyed the mandate of his tyrannical lord from fear, not inclination) stood on the altar-steps; and before him knelt the afflicted victim for mercy, her unnatural persecutor forcibly retaining her, and gazing on her, with malicious triumph. And now, the priest had rehearsed part of the awful ceremony, and Rodorigo was attempting to force the fatal ring upon his cousin's finger; when a loud shout was heard: the folding doors were burst open, and a troop of archers, with Don

Hannibal and an Alguazil at their head, rushed into the chapel.

"That is your prisoner," said the old soldier, pointing to Rodorigo, who assumed a lofty air, and demanded to know of what he was accused.

"Of murder—of parricide!" replied the veteran. "You may well start, unnatural wretch! for we shall produce your accomplice, anon. A detachment of you,"—turning to the guards—"go to a cottage that stands south of the castle, at the distance of a league, and take into custody a ruffian, who inhabits it, known by the name of Volponé."

"Behold him here, ready to answer to the charge!" said one of the archers, stepping from the ranks and throwing off his uniform.

CHAP. IX.

This is the man should do the bloody deed—
The image of a wicked heinous fault
Lives in his eye———

KING JOHN.[1]

Mistake me not for my complexion—
THE MERCHANT OF VENICE.[2]

THE person of Volponé filled his spectators with sentiments of prejudice not much in his favour. He was a raw-boned man, with one shoulder higher than the other. His countenance was particularly striking; for besides a strong squint, his complexion was of a dingy olive, his eye-brows black and penthouse; his mouth wide, with very few teeth, and those long and black; a nose like a negro's, and

1 Shakespeare, *King John* (1623), 4.2.69-71.
2 Shakespeare, *The Merchant of Venice* (1600), 2.1.1.

a peaked chin. Add to this several conspicuous scars on his visage, and this is a precise picture of him.

Rodorigo's cheek turned pale, when he saw him; but he affected a contemptuous silence, while the Alguazil declared the sacred place they were in, was ill-calculated to take evidence on a charge of murder; and telling the accused he must accompany them, they repaired to the great hall.

There the general proceeded to impart to Volponé the danger he stood in, as the accomplice of Rodorigo.

"This letter," added he, "assures me you are implicated in the business, and that a witness will be forth-coming, to make it as plain as a pikestaff."

"I shall not put you to the trouble of producing any other evidence *on my account*, Signor," replied he: "nor will you, I imagine, deem it necessary, when I confess that *I* am the author of that letter, and am ready to make a statement of such facts as will startle the steadiest mind."

The Alguazil took a pen and ink, and copied the deposition of Volponé—which he delivered in the following words:

"I was born at Leon; and at an early age, left sole master of a good estate, which I soon contrived to squander in gaming, drinking, and all manner of debauchery. My patrimony being exhausted, I entered into a society of wretches, who availed themselves of the credulous, and robbed them at play.

"We had made several booties by this nefarious practice, (which were as quickly expended) when an inquiry into our conduct was threatened by the police. I had a peculiar aversion to the galleys, and had made up my mind to cut with the community, when chance threw me into the society of Don Rodorigo de Henares.

"*He was charmed with the openness of my countenance*, and

judging that I possessed a heart congenial with his own, he made advances towards an acquaintance, and hinted (if I would be faithful to him) he would provide for me: bit by the sharp fang of poverty. I consented, and received fifty pistoles as earnest of my hellish hire.

"The first of my employments was to procure a picklock, to open a cabinet, belonging to the count; the blame of which was to be thrown on Don Torrismond, while his brother and myself were to enjoy the profits, which were considerable. Signor Torrismond had been engaged in a duel, and had it was feared (though it proved otherwise) mortally wounded his opponent; in the height of his remorse he addressed his father, and the horror he expressed at the enormity of his crime, (*the disclosure whereof, he left to his brother*) was, by the wily Rodorigo, converted into compunction for having committed the theft—whereas, worthy young man!—*he did not know of it!*

"The count said he would instantly send him his forgiveness; when the artful Rodorigo persuaded his father not to write himself, but to leave it to him—and instead of comforting his afflicted brother with the intelligence of his parent's pardon, he informed him, he had his curses!"

Don Hannibal groaned, and struck his crutch upon the floor.

"Moreover," continued Volponé, "a common courtezan was employed to keep up the farce, who waited on the old count, and represented his elder son as her seducer; in short, nothing was omitted that was likely to turn the mind of a virtuous father against an abandoned child.

"I soon after attended Don Rodorigo to Toledo whither he went to conduct his cousin from a convent. He said he was in love with her, and as he had no hope of gaining her by fair means, he instructed two of us to wait for him, in a certain street, as he passed with the lady at night, and to force her from him. This, he said, would be a plausible way of accounting for her disappearance; and we were to convey her to a dismal house, near the city, where he was to visit her at his leisure, and if noting else availed, force was to complete his purpose.

"We executed part of our commission in taking the lady from him, but a brave cavalier met, attacked, and forced us to give up our prey.

"Not long after, we returned hither; and I, by my employer's order, purchased a cottage in the neighbourhood. The next business I was concerned for him in was this: I attended him one evening, at the castle; when (having extorted a promise not to betray him) he told me, that particular circumstances rendered the *removal* of one of his father's guests necessary. That he, (whom he called Don Carlos) had dared to rival him in the affections of his cousin, Signora Aurora; and that, moreover, he was the man who had rescued her at Toledo—for which I ought to owe him no good will. He added, that his revenge would not be completed by the death of Carlos; but that he would blacken his memory—the plan of which he had already in embryo by sowing dissension between that cavalier and one Don Hilario. 'I will leave the private door, that opens into the vaulted passage, open,' said he: 'you and Bazil (your confederate) must enter his room at midnight; take him to some distance, and poniard him—but do not forget to hide the body, and to bring me his scarf and dagger, for which I have an use.'

"I promised obedience," continued Volponé, "but without any intention of keeping my word.

"I went with my confederate to Don Carlos' apartment, where we bound him in his sleep; we then gagged him, and conveyed him to my cottage. There releasing him, I disclosed my commission, but disguised the name of my employer and told him there was no way to save his life, but by his binding himself, in a solemn oath, to do what I required. He hesitated, and talked of honour. I answered, I should demand nothing which could affect him in that point; and in fine, the love of life prevailed on him to give the oath that he would immediately depart from the neighbourhood of Henares, nor make known to any one what had transpired between us. I then bade him adieu, having taken from him his dagger and scarf—both of which I conveyed to Rodorigo; who informed me, he had in the interim assassinated Don Hilario, and would contrive to make it appear the work of Don Carlos. I heard of the murder with horror: and departed with a fixed purpose of cancelling all further intercourse with such a blood-thirsty wretch, so soon as I had obtained the promised reward.

"As if he had not waded deep enough in sin, his next exploit was on the life of his own father!—I wonder not to see ye start.—I was employed by him to procure *a composing draught, which was to rid him of the old fool!* such were his words.

"I should have told you, that the child brought hither by Don Carlos, is son to the Marchioness of Valencia, and that the *amiable* Signor Rodorigo is the father!—that it was exposed on the mountains by Leonarda, at the desire of its *affectionate* parents, where it was found by Don Carlos; who was near meeting his death, as the reward of his benevolence, the very night of his arrival. Leonarda listened to his conversation with old Lewis, and reported it to Rodorigo; he entered the stranger's room to assassinate him, but his intended victim made him, coward-like, retreat precipitately.

"Further, that the late Marquis of Valencia was taken off by poison, procured by Don Rodorigo, and administered by his wife—who was herself murdered by the hand of her accomplice. I advertised Signora Rodorigo of the stratagem laid for her by Don Rodorigo, and sent the marchioness in her stead, to the cottage—little thinking how melancholy the catastrophe could prove.

"Thus you have had an enumeration of the *virtues* of Signor Rodorigo, Count de Henares; and what says the Count to my relation?" concluded Volponé.

Rodorigo replied:

"He saw the whole was a plot (but a very shallow one) to traduce his fair character; and when the only witness against him was one, by his own words, no better than a needy sharper, he should not deign to answer the charge.

"That you must do, in another place," observed the officer.

"And if he objects to *my* evidence, I can produce one who will silence *all* his objections," replied Volponé. "Will you, Signor Alguazil, suffer two or more of your men to accompany me a little way, and I will return within two hours, to prove my words?"

The officer ordered four of the band to attend him; and he returned within the limited time, conducting an object that froze the blood in Rodorigo's veins—it was his father!

"Betrayed! betrayed!" screamed the horror-stricken villain, averting his face. "Spirits quit their graves to criminate me, and the tenants of hell thunder in my ears—*Murderer! Parricide!*—pshaw! it was illusion.—Ah! no (gazing on the emaciated figure of the Count) it is accomplished: when an injured father's spirit rises from the dead, a damning evidence against a guilty son, 'twere vain to contend with fate.—I confess all!"—

"Hold!" interrupted the Count, "condemn not yourself: I *forgive* all; and a life of contrition may obtain *God's* forgiveness."

"It rests with me to interfere, my lord," said the officer.

"Though the voice of nature may stifle resentment in *your* bosom, the atrocious acts with which your son stands charged, demand cognizance of the law—whose officer I am. I shall bear him to Seville, and deliver him to the power of the inquisition. The king is there; and, if crimes like his are to pass with impunity, a father's petition will be the most likely means of averting his fate.—Do not address me on the subject, my lord;" (perceiving the afflicted count was about to speak) "I must, I *will* do my duty."

All the unhappy father could obtain in his son's behalf was, that he should remain at the castle under guard, till the next day; when he, himself, fixed to accompany him to Seville, and plead for his pardon. It being near dawn, the count was prevailed on to retire; which he did, after tenderly embracing his unnatural son.

Now to account for Antonio's appearance, after being supposed dead.

Rodorigo had employed his agent to get him a dose of poison, to destroy the count; but Volponé could not connive at murder, much less parricide, and gave him a strong opiate, in lieu, which operated for many hours; and the terror of Rodorigo, lest he should be detected, made him hasten the funeral of his father, and better answered Volponé's end. The last had disclosed the matter to the superior of the monastery, where the corpse was to be interred; and they, after the ceremony, removed it to a warm bed, and restored animation. The old Count had since resided at the convent, walking, when dark, to the abode of his preserver, for the benefit of the air, and absolutely refusing to assert his rights for the recovery of his estates, or to take any measures which would criminate Rodorigo in the eye of the world.

It was during one of his visits to the cottage, that Rodorigo had murdered the marchioness; which diabolical act drew involuntary exclamations from Antonio, (who had concealed himself) by his guilty son, deemed supernatural.

Volponé was caressed by all, and proved, that however unfavourable the exterior, a good heart may beat within— as a paltry casket often contains a jewel of immense value.

CHAP. X.

————Last scene of all,
That ends this strange eventful history————
AS YOU LIKE IT.[1]

IT was only a few days after the arrival of Don Antonio at Seville, whither he was accompanied by his brother Hannibal, and Signora Aurora, that he was informed two travelling musicians were at the gate, and craved admission for the night. The count, as well as the whole family, was in dejection, and it was agreed to admit them, hoping their minstrelsy might chase away an heavy hour, or two. They entered; and being desired to give a taste of their skill, the young one touched his lute, and sung the pangs of hopeless love; he then described the transports arising from a mutual affection, and lastly, painted the horrors of a sudden separation from the idol of the heart. During this last strain, his voice became so tremulous as to be scarcely articulate; and 'ere the end, Aurora, in whose breast it excited a mingle sensation of pain and pleasure, burst into tears, and would have fallen from her seat, had not the youthful minstrel ran, and caught her in his arms.— Presently she turned to chide his presumption, when he threw off his cloak, and the well-remembered person of

1 2.7.162-163.

Carlos stood confessed—Carlos, whose supposed depravity and death, she had successively deplored.—The lady beheld her lover with equal joy and astonishment, having imagined him buried in the cave belonging to the banditti; Don Hannibal grasped his hand, and protested he had known no such happiness since last he smelt powder—in short, he was cordially welcomed by all.

Carlos introduced his companion (an elegant cavalier of fifty) by the name of Don Alphonso; then addressed his auditors thus:—

"You will, haply, wish to know the cause of my withdrawing myself from the castle so abruptly, and what has befallen me since. In those particulars I shall be happy to satisfy you."

They imparted to him the confession of Volponé; on which, Carlos took up the story, from the time he parted with him at the cottage.

"Having pledged my oath, (than which nothing can be dearer to a Spaniard) I determined strictly to adhere to it," said he, "and made the best of my way for the royal camp; in my road to which, I was stripped of every thing by robbers—even of a favourite ring, (casting a look at Aurora) which I prized as my own life. On reaching the army, a detachment was ordered by forced marches, to surprise the Moorish camp before Granada; but they had intimation of the design, and the advanced party were slain, or captured.

"Mahomet Boabdilli Chequito, the Moorish king, affected great rage at what he called the perfidy of the Christian dogs, and swore he would not spare one of them, but gave orders for a general massacre.

"The subsequent morning was appointed for the execution of this hellish mandate; but the troops of Ferdinand, with the invincible Gonsalvo de Cordova at their head, assaulted the city in the interval, and the rising sun, which was to have witnessed the slaughter of thousands of our Redeemer's disciples, beheld the Christian banners float, triumphant, on the walls of Granada.

"I had the good fortune to save the life of Don Alphonso, at the minute the bow-string was round his neck, and who had lingered sixteen years of misery in a noisome dungeon. I prevailed on him to accompany me to Seville, where we arrived yesterday; and hearing Count Henares was in the city, I have waited on him, to pay my respects."

"I am glad to see you," said Hannibal; "but why not come like yourself? why fight under false colours?"

"Enough, brother," interrupted the Count, "Don Carlos you are welcome to me, and all my roof affords—I have some time desired your presence. But to the point. I wish to render others happy, though I can never more be so myself. Does your passion for my niece still exist?"

"It does, with increased ardour," cried Carlos.

"Then she is yours," quoth the Count; "and if you can prevail on her, your nuptials shall be celebrated three days from this."

Carlos pressed the Count's proposal with such fervor, that the beauteous Aurora gave her consent with a blush; and Don Alphonso said:

"Then I shall have the pleasure of seeing my deliverer happy. I have property to no small amount in Spain, which I should never have claimed on my own account; but it shall be his—and every joy attend him, and his lovely choice!"

The ceremony was performed at the stated time, to the great delight of Carlos, who thought all his past anxiety amply rewarded by the fair hand of his Aurora.

But, alas! how short-lived is all earthly happiness!—Like water-bubbles, which vanish almost as soon as they appear.

On the afternoon of the desired day, a cavalier was thrown from his horse, at the gate of the Count's residence, and broke his leg. He was conveyed to a chamber in the palace, and the fracture being of a compound nature, he was informed the only chance of saving his life would be by submitting to an amputation. In the mean time, the Count, Alphonso, and Carlos went to visit him; and the invalid no sooner cast his eyes on the last, than he exclaimed—

"Carlos!"

"My father!" returned the other, with equal admiration.

"Ah!" cried the stranger, observing Don Alphonso, "you here, Marquis Almanza? Then the hand of heaven is in it indeed!"

"Don Gomez!" said Alphonso.

"Yes, the guilty Gomez: but do not curse me, when you shall know my villainy. I left my home in search of Carlos, and Providence has inflicted my present calamity, to bring me to your presence, that I may make some reparation for the ills I have done you.

"When you, Marquis, departed for the wars (some seventeen years ago) and left your wife, together with an infant son and daughter, in my charge, I had all good will to fulfil the sacred trust reposed in me. But when your letter told me, you were made prisoner by the Moors, and that a large sum only would release you (which I was ordered to remit) the damned thought first struck me, to take advantage of the power you had given me over your estates; and I returned you answer, that your wife was gone off with a grandee, for the new world—taking your children with her. As I prognosticated, you sent no reply; and I concluded (not without a heartfelt-triumph) the hateful intelligence had ended you. Your wife I confined in the ruins of a priory, adjoining my own castle; using every other precaution to preserve my fatal secret, that human foresight could suggest. Your son I reared as my own, and there he stands."

"Am I so blest?" cried the Marquis Almanza, throwing himself on Carlos' neck. "To find a son in my preserver, is gratifying, indeed. But does my wife still survive?"

"She does," answered Gomez; "or, rather, she exists— for living you cannot call it, to be immured as she is."

"And my daughter?"

"Your daughter I dropt at the door of a nobleman, at Burgos; his name Antonio, Count de Henares—"

"Recall your words; I am Antonio de Henares," exclaimed the Count.—"Was it the sister of Carlos who was laid at my door some sixteen years ago?"

"The same," replied Gomez.

"Almighty God!" cried Antonio, "then Carlos is the husband of his own sister!"

"Heaven forbid!" cried the guilty Gomez, shuddering.

"I fear it is too true," returned the Count; "that child I have reared as my own niece—and Carlos has espoused her.—But not to leave the shadow of a doubt, was not the infant wrapt in a blue mantle?"

"It was; and I have the curse of incest added to the catalogue of my crimes. After having separated those whom heaven had joined—dooming one to slavery in an infidel country, and the other to solitary captivity—while I exposed their daughter to the chance of perishing for want—and meditated the death of their son, for having, as I thought, been too inquisitive—the measure of my sins, if filled with incest, of which I have been the cause.—Hell has no part hot enough for such a wretch as I am!"

He was informed that he had not the last crime to answer for; but the intelligence seemed to afford him little consolation, and he died in a raging fever—having previously given necessary instructions to the Marquis Almanza, to liberate his long-lost wife.

That nobleman's son, the unfortunate Carlos, deprived

of the happiness he had promised himself (in being bereft of Aurora) and shocked at his proximity to a crime at which nature shudders, accompanied his late-found father on the occasion—hoping, in his loved society, to find a balsam for his wounded mind.

About this period, a rumour was spread through Seville, that Ricardo (the famous robber) was in captivity; a reward of five hundred crowns was set on his head, and a free pardon to his band, would they bring him in, dead or alive. Disgusted with his mode of life, and anxious to insure the lives of his adherents, he summoned his band; they formed themselves into a semicircle, and leaning on their arms, regarded him attentively, as with a solemn voice, he thus addressed them:

"Brothers—attend to what I am about to say, nor let a mistaken sense of duty, or generosity, prevent your deciding according to the dictates of prudence; weigh the advantages you will forego, by a refusal of my proposal, and at the same time, that you will be wandering each day, farther from the path of heaven. Behold this paper: it proclaims pardon and freedom to you all, for merely giving me up to death—who am willing to purchase your lives, at the price of my blood, spilt on a public scaffold.

"Do you hesitate? If you accede, you are offered liberty and life, and, on the other hand, what can you expect should you ultimately escape corporeal punishment, but infamy and curses?—

"No answer yet?—Perhaps you think of dying in the field, like heroes.—Robbers cannot hope it; they must tremble at death—while the innocent blood they have shed, withers the laurel that else might grow for them.

"What, still irresolute?—For shame! for shame! assume some manhood, one of you, and say, who is the first to save his fellows, by giving up his captain?"

"If hell should stare him in the face," cried one, "damned be the dog that would betray or abandon him!"

Ricardo used many other arguments, but all to no effect, on which, he secretly repaired to the nearest magistrate, and told him he came to give up the robber-chieftain; but first required a verbal repetition, that the lives of the banditti should be indemnified.

This, the magistrate readily agreed to, and demanded where the captain was to be found.

"You see him now;" replied Ricardo, with composure.

The magistrate appeared in alarm at this intelligence, and summoned his Myrmidons presently—not thinking himself safe in the presence of Ricardo, whom he considered capable of any deed, however atrocious.

Ricardo was put into a close carriage, accompanied by three officers of police, and conveyed to Seville, where he was delivered up to the Inquisition.

He was confined in a frightful dungeon of free-stone, arched, and so gloomy, that the only light it received was through a grated window, about one foot square, and situated at least ten feet from the floor.

In this dismal place, subsisting on black bread and unwholesome water, did the wretched Ricardo continue three weeks, during which period no human voice saluted his ear, save the complaints, dismal cries, and hollow groans of other prisoners, echoing through this dreadful mansion; and which the otherwise solemn silence made still more shocking. Time seemed to have lost all motion, and these few days appeared to him like so many years.

On the twenty-second day, he was ordered to appear before the holy office. When brought before them, his courage failed him not; he entered the hall with a firm step and undaunted mien. The president, who with four inquisitors, was there, bade him kneel down, lay his right hand on the bible, and swear, in the presence of Almighty God, that he would answer truly, whatever questions might be put to him.

"First," demanded Ricardo, "pledge yourselves in the same sacred manner, to fulfil the conditions of your proclamation, with regard to my followers. That done, I shall answer freely."

"Son, son," said the president, "both they and you have been woeful sinners, not only in theft and murder, but in speaking injuriously of the holy office, as we are well assured. It therefore becomes you as a catholic and a penitent, to disclose their abode, and accuse them of the crimes they have committed.—In doing this, you will excite compassion of this tribunal, which is ever merciful to those who speak the truth."

"Then you recant the promise to preserve their lives?" cried Ricardo.

"We do," replied the president; "were their crimes forgiven till the day of retribution, heaven would not fail to inflict some damning punishment upon them: their sufferings here may haply appease the supreme being, and be the passport to absolution. Finally, we but obey an order from above, in dooming them to death; blush then, to plead for wretches like them."

"Blush for yourselves, not me!" retorted Ricardo. "Faithless men! who having lured me to this state in the fond hope of saving those brave fellows, whom lately I commanded, break through all solemn promises, all sacred ties, yet dare profanely to call yourselves the ministers of justice!"

"Insolent!" cried one of the inquisitors, "this from an acknowledged robber. But torture shall tame this stubborn courage, and damp your moralizing pride."

"Hear me, I will *now* speak proudly," said Ricardo, in a

voice that commanded attention—"and tell ye, supreme powers of this merciless tribunal (whose breath bears with it death in lingering tortures) I am no thief, who conspires with midnight to fright the tender mother and her lisping infant from the lap of sleep. What I have done, I shall no doubt, find registered hereafter—but with you, bloodthirsty men! I will not waste more words, than to assure you, I never will betray my comrades. Your offer of life upon such terms, would to the happy be a worthless tender; what must it be to me then, who wish to die?—I am prepared to meet your malice: inflict your tortures, practise unheard of cruelties upon me—you cannot shake my constancy, or make me tremble."

"Take him away;" cried they—"we shall find means to tame this lion.—To his dungeon with him."

Three days subsequent, he was ordered before the court again; and as he persisted in refusing to disclose the haunt of his band, he was conducted to the torture-room.

This was a spacious apartment, built in the form of a square tower, and partially lighted by two dim lamps; and to prevent the groans and shrieks of the unhappy victims from reaching the ears of their fellow-prisoners, the doors were lined within and without.

On a sudden he was surrounded by six wretches, who stript him to his drawers, and threw him on his back upon the scaffold.—They put an iron collar round his neck, which was fastened to the stage, and a ring of the same metal being affixed to each ankle, they stretched him till every limb cracked. All this while no murmur of complaint escaped him; all he uttered was:—

"Oh! Father of mercy! deign to accept my expiation!"

They then proceeded to wind a rope round each arm, and one round each thigh, which ropes passed under the scaffold, through holes made for that purpose. These ropes were at a signal given, drawn tight by four men; and being no thicker than a man's little finger, cut through the flesh quite to the bone, making a stream of blood issue from the four different places that were thus bound.— Still he endured it without a groan. They next placed an enormous weight upon his chest; adding more and more till the excessive pressure forced the blood from his eyes, nose, and mouth, and he became insensible—insomuch that he was carried back to his dungeon, without perceiving it.

His sufferings were not to end here; he was sentenced to the stake, and doomed to suffer at the approaching Auto de Fé.

At length, the fatal day arrived: the officers of the Inquisition, preceded by trumpets and other martial music, marched to the great square, where a scaffold was raised. Multitudes of people appeared, as splendidly attired as for a royal wedding; and for some hours came prisoners of either sex.

The whole court was present; and amongst the rest, the Count Henares, whose duty to his sovereign called him thither.—Many criminals were bound to the stake, when a buz of voices cried:—

"Here he comes—here comes the famous captain of the banditti—Ricardo!"

Antonio requested a nobleman near him, to point out the man; he complied, when the count from the balcony, rushed to the scaffold, struck the torch from the executioner's hand, as he was about to set fire to the faggots, and throwing himself on the shoulder of the prisoner, exclaimed:—"My son! my son!"

He entreated the executioner to pause only for ten minutes, while he addressed his Majesty; then rushed to the foot of the throne, with all the agility of youth, and prostrated himself before the royal Ferdinand.

"Never, Sire, never will I rise," said the venerable parent, in a voice almost drowned in sobs, "till you forgive yon man.—It is my son, Torrismond, (once the pride of my heart) for whom I sue. Oh! royal Isabella! plead for him— save me from another pang; nor let me be left childless in my old age, like a blighted tree, stript of its spreading branches. Pardon, oh! king! or let me die with him!"

Ferdinand and his consort were moved to tears: he told him, his suit was granted, raised him from the ground, and gave orders for the release of Torrismond (late Ricardo) who was, once more, restored to his fond father's arms; and warmly welcomed home by Hannibal and Aurora— the latter of whom recounted his generous behaviour to her, while in the cave belonging to the banditti.

A fortnight had elapsed, when the Marquis Almanza returned to Seville, bringing with him his suffering wife, the amiable Ximena, and a young female, the latter of whom Aurora recollected to be Rosa, the girl who had so hospitably entertained her in her flight from Henares Castle—though she was now richly dressed.

"Allow me," said Carlos to Aurora, taking the young female by the hand, "to present my sister to you: though, from your mutual surprise, I should suppose you are no strangers."

Aurora related the manner of their becoming acquainted, but confessed herself incredulous as to the assertion of Rosa's being his sister.

"It is true indeed; and I will briefly tell you, how I came in possession of this valuable treasure—" observed the Marquis, pressing the young stranger to his heart. "In our journey to the castle of Don Gomez, we halted for the night, at a neat cottage, and here Carlos, as had been the case all the way, was bewailing his cruel destiny, in depriving him of Aurora. 'And the Count Henares,' continued he, 'why did he not declare she was not his niece?'

"At these words, an old woman (whom I supposed mother to this dear girl, and who was in the room) threw herself on her knees, and begged forgiveness for her duplicity—to which she had been instigated by the devil. I was at a loss to comprehend her meaning—but she soon explained herself, by informing me—Count Henares had placed an infant niece called Aurora, to be reared by her; that she had a daughter of the same age, and the opportunity of providing well for her, induced her to make an exchange of the children; which she did—sending her own at seven years of age to the Count, and retaining his niece as hers. Her conscience, she said, often smote her, and when Carlos coupled the names of Henares and Aurora, she found it impossible to preserve her secret longer.

'Forgive me, that I have passed my own child on the Count, as his niece, and restore this young creature to him, (presenting her supposed daughter) for she is the true Aurora. God has converted my heart; and I am ready to make oath as to what I have said.'—

"Together with my new-found children, I pursued my journey, and liberated the wife of my bosom from the confinement in which she had lingered sixteen long years, by the vile machinations of the worthless Don Gomez—and it shall be the study of her happy husband to obliterate all past sufferings from her memory, and to gild the autumn of her days with every earthly pleasure.

"Thus you see, (addressing himself to the beloved of Carlos) you are not my child, nor any longer Aurora; but I am right willing to bestow Rosa (for that is your *real* name) on my dear son, and consequently to receive you as my daughter-in-law."

Each one was emulous to evince satisfaction at

the sudden revolution in the fortunes of the house of Almanza. Ximena, (spite of sufferings, a lovely ruin) was, unexpectedly restored to a fond husband, who had himself experienced the horrors of captivity. Aurora (*late Rosa*) was suddenly raised from poverty to an exalted rank, and Carlos was blest with the hand of his adored Rosa.

They retired to the castle of Almanza, taking with him the orphan son of Rodorigo and Philippa; to whom Carlos (in pursuance of his vow) became a parent. A numerous progeny of their own blest their retirement, and amused the declining hours of the faithful Lewis—who accompanied his young mistress, and breathed his last under her roof.

The Count's care, during his sojourn at Seville, had been to prefer his petition, in favour of Rodorigo, to King Ferdinand—but the nature of his crimes had been fully stated to his Majesty, who was deaf to supplication.

The distressed father passed much of his time with his worthless son—striving to comfort him with every argument reason and religion could suggest. They were however lost upon him: the arrogance with which he had at first sustained the charge against him was converted into cowardice, and he besought his father to save his life—though it were to be ended in his present dungeon.

"Save me!" would the dastardly wretch cry, "oh! save me, father! from the claws of the inquisitors, and let me be buried alive, in the very centre of the earth!"

This disgrace to nature paid the price of his crimes by a punishment, that nothing but the heinousness of his offences could justify; and which was delayed till after the celebration of the Auto de Fé, to render it more exemplary.

His sentence was to be confined with six half-starved cats, in an iron cage, suspended over a slow-fire. This doom he endured in the presence of a vast crowd of spectators—who answered his shrieks with loud shouts and bitter exclamations.

Meanwhile, the repentant Torrismond, in opposition to the entreaties of his friends, retired to a monastery, whither he was accompanied by his father; and when they bade adieu to those they left behind, the former quitted them with these words:

"Come round, and take my parting embrace; and when in future days you may mourn my lot, let it be a warning to you and yours, to shun vice, when it approaches in the seductive garb of pleasure. There was the cause of my first lapse from right. Still, all might have been well, had it not been for one—but he is gone to his account. The son of my father has bereft me of heaven—but I forgive him!" He paused, and wiped a starting tear from his eye; then proceeded:

"When your supposed malediction, my father, reached me—Oh! God!—how trifling were the corporeal pangs I late endured, to what I then felt about my heart?—Oh, thought I, when love is banished from a parent's breast, turn heart to tiger, and let every nerve distort itself with savage fury!—Cursed be the world! myself! and all mankind! man renounced humanity to me, when I appealed to it; therefore, hence all sympathy and forbearance! I'll henceforth league with murderers and robbers," (his auditors shuddered) "and be as the avenging sword of the Almighty, to all evil doers! With that erroneous thought, was all law trampled beneath my feet. I sought to relieve the indigent, protect the oppressed, redress the injured, and punish the oppressor————but I was an enthusiast!— With my own hand (oh! father! do not gaze upon me!) I slew a monopolizer, rolling in riches, obtained at the price of his fellow-creature's misery; many tears flowed from the hungry, on his account. I assassinated a worthless priest for lamenting in his pulpit, that the Inquisition was held in disrepute—and all as the agent of heaven.—Fool! fool! soon dropt the bandage from my eyes!—soon did my heart convince me of the fallacy of my hopes—soon did I feel myself despised by that power, of whom I had arrogantly deemed myself the minister. No monuments perpetuate the actions of banditti—their victories are hailed with curses, danger, death, and shame.

"Farewel! we shall meet again, in another world.—I now hasten from the eyes of men; and will conceal myself in a monastic cell, where even the light of day shall shrink back at my infamy!"

FINIS.

APPENDIX

Review of John Palmer, Jun.'s stage acting at the Hay-Market Theatre

We are sorry to see this young man still pursuing a profession, for which, neither in form or talent, nature ever designed him. His figure is stiff and meagre, his features harsh, his voice inharmonious, and his gestures stiff. That, on account of his father's merits, the public should countenance him, is an amiable trait in the British audience; but he should be kept to subordinate parts, and not act such characters as he performs in the Iron Chest, and many other pieces. It is mistaken lenity in reviewers to pass over the glaring defects of young actors, to forbear telling them that their genius does not tend to make them proficient in stage excellence, at a period of their life, when, with a little trouble, they may turn their thoughts to other means of gaining an honourable livelihood.

—*Monthly Literary Recreations*, July 1807, pp. 114-115.

Bibliography of John Palmer, Jun. (1776-1809)

The Haunted Cavern: A Caledonian Tale. London: B. Crosby, 1795.

The Mystery of the Black Tower. London: Printed for the author by William Lane at the Minerva Press, 1796.

The World as it Goes; *or, Portraits from Nature*. London: Moore and Beauclerc, 1803.

The Mystic Sepulchre; *or, Such Things Have Been. A Spanish Romance*. London: W. Earle, 1806.

Like Master Like Man: A Novel. London: W. Earle, 1811.